CHANGING THE FACE
OF CANADIAN LITERATURE

ESSENTIAL ANTHOLOGIES SERIES 12

Guernica Editions Inc. acknowledges the support of the Canada Council
for the Arts and the Ontario Arts Council. The Ontario Arts Council
is an agency of the Government of Ontario.

We acknowledge the financial support of the Government of Canada.

CHANGING THE FACE
OF CANADIAN LITERATURE

Compiled and edited by
Dane Swan

GUERNICA
EDITIONS

GUERNICA
TORONTO – BUFFALO – LANCASTER (U.K.)
2020

Editor: Dane Swan
Book Cover and Layout: Alvin Wong
General Editor: Michael Mirolla
Cover image: Kiki Zhang
Guernica Editions Inc.
287 Templemead Drive, Hamilton (ON), Canada L8W 2W4
2250 Military Road, Tonawanda, N.Y. 14150-6000 U.S.A.
www.guernicaeditions.com

Distributors:
University of Toronto Press Distribution, 5201 Dufferin Street, Toronto (ON), Canada M3H 5T8
Gazelle Book Services, White Cross Mills, High Town, Lancaster LA1 4XS U.K.
Independent Publishers Group (IPG), 600 North Pulaski Road, Chicago IL 60624

First edition.
Printed in Canada.

Legal Deposit - Third Quarter

Library of Congress Catalog Card Number: 2019945610
Library and Archives Canada Cataloguing in Publication
Title: Changing the face of Canadian literature / compiled and edited by Dane Swan.
Names: Swan, Dane, editor.
Description: Series statement: Essential anthologies series ; 12
Identifiers: Canadiana (print) 20190153385 | Canadiana (ebook) 20190153725
| ISBN 9781771835237 (softcover) | ISBN 9781771835244 (EPUB) | ISBN 9781771835251 (Kindle)
Subjects: LCSH: Ethnic groups—Canada—Literary collections.
| CSH: Canadian literature (English)—Minority authors. | CSH: Canadian literature (English)—21st century.
Classification: LCC PS8235.M56 C43 2020 | DDC C810.8/09206930971—dc23

table of contents

table of contents

02

table of contents

table of contents

03

table of contents

table of contents

04

table of contents

table of contents

table of contents

table of contents

foreword

As a young reader, the one thing that I always hated in books were long forewords. Now as an adult, and the editor of this anthology, this places me in a peculiar predicament. There's a lot to say. A lot that needs to be put out there about what Canada aspires to be and how its literary and arts communities, as a whole, have failed to recognize those aspirations in the work that is held up as Canada's triumphant creative output. I can't ignore that because I once hated reading long forewords. Hopefully, my younger self will forgive my transgression.

I write this from my apartment in Toronto, a city that celebrates trade and diverse cultures—despite the actions of certain groups in its recent past. Toronto inhabits Tkaronto, a place of trade and diverse indigenous nations including the Wendat, Anishinaabeg, Haudenosaunee, and Mississauga of the New Credit. It's almost as if the land is telling us how to live here. To trade both products and knowledge. To attempt to live peacefully in an environment born of many nations.

Since the 60's, Canada has aspired to be a multicultural nation—almost as if the aspirations of Canada, began to reflect the history of the region of Turtle Island it inhabits. However in literature, the recognition of authors from non Anglo Saxon cultures (in more than a token manner) until the last decade, has been abysmal.

Yes, there have been great authors like Austin Clarke, but even he did not get any real recognition from the literary elite in Canada until the 90's. Furthermore, Rinaldo Walcott's refusal to be a part of the "Can-Lit" scene is well documented. Even the press that has published this book, Guernica Editions, likely does not exist if it wasn't for Italian-Canadian writers not being recognized as writers by those who benefit from a glass ceiling.

I could go on, how the UBC Creative Writing Program controversy was handled by some of Canada's literary elite, drew a clear line to many of Canada's authors. As did the swell of racists who took joy from the controversy that took place at *Write Magazine*. The ease and comfort that editors and writers at some of Canada's most vaunted magazines and publications flaunted their hate was discouraging.

That said, things are better than they were. Back in 2009, when Guernica Editions offered to publish my first book, *Bending the Continuum*, I tried to research the literary landscape for black Canadian writers. Back then, most of the black authors I met waited until they were 40, and had a post grad degree before attempting to get published. Those who didn't want to wait migrated to the US, or self-published. The exception being a small pool of authors who were published in Ayanna Black's *Voices* anthology.

Currently, most black authors still feel obligated to get post grad degrees, but they're getting them at younger ages. Despite black men disproportionately not getting into post grad creative writing programs in Canada, a larger portion of those who do leave for the US are returning. I no longer feel isolated when I go to literary events in Toronto. There are more people of diverse backgrounds in more rooms, and in more roles. We still need more agents, more editors, and more people in positions of power from disenfranchised communities, but in a very short period of time I have been able to physically see things change as more culturally diverse faces enter the literary scene.

But I must digress, this anthology does not celebrate multiculturalism, it celebrates diversity. Diversity is a far wider spectrum. Diversity recognizes those both franchised and disenfranchised. Diversity includes those able and differently able. Diversity recognizes the geography of Canada. Despite rumors to the contrary, Canada is not a Toronto monolith. There are fantastic authors and poets in other cities, towns and provinces. Diversity recognizes that new writing can be written by both the young and the young at heart. Diversity recognizes that an author may identify as male, female, or other. Diversity also acknowledges that not all writers seek the page as their primary medium.

It's not who you know, it's the quality of your writing, and how you engage your readers that matters. It's not about writing work that fits in, it's about writing work that stands out because of an author's unique quirks and their perspective shaped by the things that make them who they are. It's not the schools the author may, or may not have gone to, it's whether the people who read their writing enjoy the experience. The more diverse a nation's writers are, the wider the breadth of people who feel they are a part of that nation. Why? Because their story is being told as part of the nation's narrative. This moment, when so many voices from people with funny faces and names are being published, gaining recognition and being praised here and abroad, is something to celebrate, not just taken for granted as it currently is.

Every historically recognized literary movement in Canada's history before now has been used to exclude voices from its literature. This can be traced back to Canada's first literary movement. The Confederation Poets (1880-1897) were Canada's first school of poets. To be a member, you had to be a poet of the right 'stock,' and considered young. Of course exceptions were made for older men, but all the women had to be young poets. None of this was necessarily stated aloud. Instead the catch all term, "technical excellence" was used.

The Confederation Poets were the first group of writers in Canada who recognized themselves as Canadian writers. Canada's first literary movement was very Anglo Saxon, white, affluent, and predominantly male. That was the Canada the Confederation Poets wanted to share to the world. Hauntingly, as The League of Canadian Poets was founded, in response to a groundswell of new arts funding in Canada, The League used similar language as the Confederation Poets. However, if your writing could exceed the imaginary standard of "technical excellence," you also had to be able to get a book-length collection of your work published from a recognized publisher.

Yes, people persevered. Publishing houses that promote the writing of Italian Canadians, Jewish Canadians, Black Canadians, Indigenous communities and others arose in reaction to the new walls constructed. Yes, The Dub Poets Collective fought to have a wider definition of what poetry is in Canada, and with that wider definition, access to arts funding expanded to more people.

Yes, in recent years organizations that have control over government funds have started to recognize self-published authors. Also, to be fair, The League has taken significant steps forward, in recent years, to accept members from diverse backgrounds. But how many classrooms in Canada teach The Dub Poets Collective as an important literary movement in Canada's history? Are we properly recognizing the achievements and positive impact on Canadian literature of those who've opened doors for all of us? If we don't, all of this diverse literature could easily go away.

Case in point, while putting this anthology together I did some very amateur research of Canadian anthologies that celebrated either diversity or disenfranchised people. The books that I discovered, that I thought may intrigue the readers of this anthology, I've shared at the end of this collection. What you'll notice from my list, and from your own sleuthing, is that we first start seeing anthologies that celebrate diverse cultures in Canada in the 80's. By the 90's there's an explosion of such anthologies. However, in the early 2000's very few appear to be published. Maybe that 10 year blip was complacency. Or maybe, certain publishers who celebrated disenfranchised communities dissolved and there was little motivation to fill that void. Needless to say, moments like now, when the hurdles to becoming a respected author are at their lowest. When the only hurdles to being published are the quality of your writing and your patience to deal with certain less and less important gatekeepers. Moments in history like this must be acknowledged and celebrated.

That's what this anthology is: It's a celebration. A moment to cry out, "Look how many of us have a voice! There are stories, and poetry in this country that are about people like me! I am not alone!"

Congratulations Canada, you finally have a literature that looks like the people who inhabit you. Do not take this moment for granted.

Dane Swan

Norma Dunning

(Published in *Annie Muktuk and Other Stories*)

Norma Dunning is a southern born and raised Inuit writer. She is a fifth-year doctoral candidate registered at the University of Alberta, Edmonton. Her doctoral work examines the intricacies of policy towards Inuit who are residing outside of their land claims areas.

Dunning writes in both prose and poetry. Her debut collection of short stories, *Annie Muktuk and Other Stories* received the Danuta Gleed Award 2018 and the Howard O'Hagan Award 2018 for best short story, as well as a bronze standing with Foreword Reviews and is being translated into French through a Montreal-based publisher.

She is currently working on her second collection of short stories, as well as Inuit-based children's stories and poetry.

Kabloona Red

Ka-b-loona-read. Kalona Red. Kelowna Red—that's it! Better stop drinking the wine before noon. It's so wonderful to feel that beautiful red liquid glide down my throat. It's like going home, all warm and wonderful. Is there really anything better than sitting at home, tanked in your very own kitchen? Husband is off up north, doing his bit for God, the Queen, and his country. The Queen—remember when she flew into Churchill? What a day—what excitement there was. We all curled up our hair, shaved our legs, donned our big parkas, and headed off to the airport. Excited to see royalty step off a small plane and wave at us all. Who cared that she stuck around for only a half an hour—she showed up didn't she? What a party we had at the Legion that night—all that old-time fiddle music, all the elders and the young people. We danced the northern lights away. It was glorious. Just a bunch of starry-eyed Eskimos.

Eskimo, now that's a word. White word. White word for white people to wrap around their pink tongues. Esquimaux. Spell it any way you want and it still comes out the same, skid row and all. I should light up another cig here. A rollie, make your own. Always make your own. The north teaches you that. Make your everything. Food, clothes, fun—much fun. Inhale. Exhale. Drag on that homemade-no-filter cig. Get the tobacco stuck between your teeth and absolutely never floss. "Ha," I mutter to the empty kitchen. Ah, the north.

I met him there. A tall strapping country boy from the south. I loved him from the minute we looked at each other. Me, a little Inuk and him the farm boy fresh from the war. He looked magnificent in his blue uniform. I would have done anything for him and I did. We drank and danced and laughed. I felt important. I felt white. Look at me, look at me with this white guy. He gave my world meaning.

We married and I got a new name. I could throw out my old name and no one would ever have to know. They would never have to know about my sisters or my mothers or my father. I could start fresh and new. I could invent a new me. I couldn't get rid of that skin color though. That was a drawback. Always long sleeves and pants. Wear a dress with dark nylons, sleep in rollers every night of your life and run red lipstick around your mouth first thing every morning, noon and night. People could assume what they wanted. I didn't have to give any details. I would be only his wife. That's all they ever had to know.

We got married 'cause I was pregnant. Oh let's have some more of that Kel Red—let that gallon jug glug-glug into my glass. Bring it to my lips, let it slide down the old pipes. Ah, that's good. Yeah, there was one thing that I was good at—learned it at school too. Young girls surrounded by all those priests and brothers and nuns. Father Mercredi was the first. Puts me in the punishment room and leaves me there, alone, like solitary. Shows up after dinner dishes have been scraped, spit on and polished. Kitchen crew is gone and there we are. He tells me to not scream, puts his sweaty palm over my mouth. Yanks down the heavy underwear—the woolen armor of the little girls.

Pushes my back up against a wall and rips into my body like a serpent. I close my eyes and tears drool down my face, snot drips from my nose. My heart pounds hard against that cold cement wall. He wiggles this way and that like a snowshoe hare stuck in a snare. The pain splits beads of panic off my forehead.

Norma Dunning 003

He's finished. Tucks his thing back under his black robe, slowly peels his hand off my mouth. Mutters to me in French to "ferme ta gueule—shush, don't talk about this." And he's gone. I hear his footsteps down the hallway. I slide down to the cement floor and sob softly. I hurt. I bleed. I don't know who to tell.

Sister Mary comes in to release me from the room. She sees the blood dripping down to my white socks. She puts her hand around my mouth too and quickly walks me to the bathroom. I try between whimpers to tell her it was Father Mercredi. She tells me to be quiet. To stay still. She leaves and comes back with a white cotton pad. She tells me that I will have this happen to me every month. I try to tell her, "NO!" She gets stern and says, "Oui, mon cher." She hands me the pad and mimes for me to place it into my bloody underwear "between da hegs." That memory makes me giggle now. I might have been nine years old. Every month—my foot.

Time for another quick shot here. The kitchen clock is reminding me of that place. Time was everything there. Yep, I had them all. All the Fathers. First Mercredi, then Father Jeudi, Father Vendredi, Samedi, and Dimanche and let's not forget the rest of the good old boys—Lundi and Mardi. I never really knew their names. I gave them the names of the days of the week. It all depended on what day they showed up. That went on for six years. Every night.

It was like word got around that place and I was sent to that room every day after school. Eventually I did have to start using that bale of cotton between my legs every month but that didn't stop them. Nah, those old Peres, they weren't about to fuss over something like that. But I learned one thing. I learned to pretend to like it. They learned that they didn't have to put their hand around my mouth anymore. I would breathe hard like a throat song, I would wiggle and I would moan softly into their ears. While they were pumping I was praying. Praying for them to burn. Praying for them to die. Praying to get myself the hell out of hell.

I figured out another thing too. Oh, let's just light a cig. I learned to get good grades. Not just any kind of good grades. I learned that if I became the smartest person in the province for French class I could get moved ahead in my school. I could be like a prisoner released on good behavior. Marks mattered and I got them. I finished high school a month before my 16th birthday. I led the province in French marks. I had become en-francaise-ized. They made a spectacle of me. They couldn't hide me anymore. They couldn't keep me in the punishment room now. The Bishop even knew about me and came to school one day to shake my hand. While he was congratulating me on this big accomplishment, I prayed for him to burn like the others. I smiled my you-go-to-hell smile and then I winked at him. I was set free.

Oh, the jug is getting empty. Shit, I shoulda bought more of this stuff. I only get to do this when he isn't around. Otherwise I have to be the white wife. The white wife with the white picket fence, white washed and white dried. Ah, Eskimo—what a nice white word.

Too young to be legally on my own I was fostered out to a French family. I had been in that place so long that I couldn't remember my mothers' faces. My sisters had been taken away from me years before. I had no idea where anyone was anymore. It didn't matter. Most days it didn't matter. I got to be in a real home, in a real house with a real older couple who took care of me like I was some sort of Inuit princess. I had my own room with my own books and dresser with a nice round mirror. I loved it.

I worked at their restaurant and I started to learn that life was not all bad. I learned to cook good and then I met him. He courted me like I mattered. Wouldn't kiss me on the first date. I changed that. We had a pile of kids. Lots of them. Wall to wall. We moved further north. Camped. Hunted. Fished. Went whaling and berry picking. We took that bundle of brats with us everywhere. Ah, it's a good life now.

You never really get over things. You just move on. Move on to laughter. Move on to being alive. Move on to growing old. And when he's not here, than you can really remember and you can have a sip of Kelowna Red and smoke all the cigs you want. After all it's the Inuit way.

A
D
A
M

P
O
T
T
L
E

Adam Pottle

Adam Pottle's writing explores the fiery beauty of Deafness and disability. He has published four books and had three plays produced. He lives in Saskatoon.

School for the Deaf

You gasp, awakened by
a bucket of cold water.

A gauzy autumn morning. A drained sunrise.
You shiver, strain to see the house
parent's fingers whipping & flicking in
the fibrous grey light—wordless yet
communicative fingers.

You wipe your face with
your sheet, bite back a sob.

The teachers always tell you to use your voice
even though you already have one.

When you speak or try
to speak, it's like laying an egg through your mouth,
like balancing a tire on your throat,
like lifting a barbell with your tongue,
hoping it doesn't tip or catch on a corner.
You must hoist your voice. Right now
you can't lift it. It's too heavy.

From what you can see

on the house parent's lips, you can't use your fingers.

When another boy picked his nose, the principal tied

his hands with rope. Could do the same for signing.

You watch your dorm mates

whose names you don't know,

even though you've been here two weeks.

In the cold dorm you watch their mouths,

hoping to find seething shapes,

hoping their teeth will strain whatever vapour words are made of,

hoping their tongues will lift & toss their words,

hoping their words will clench before you.

Their words slide like arrogant ghosts

through the fibrous dormitory air.

After class,

you practice mouth movements before the mirror,

trying to build your voice's muscle, pushing against

the words, as though they might bury you alive.

You see the house parent's thick digits—

knuckles furred like a tarantula's knees ,   ,

the shrill dorm light fattening the fat hairs,

spidery hands seeking to measure, seize, grasp, coax, convince.

The house parent a dull husky man
who laughs like a wolverine,
toothy laughter carried by a thrusting jaw
meant to ward you off.

You can't believe that
a real person's laughter
can be so hostile.

*

Speaking in class is
chewing vegetables
grown in a cave:

the words clack
against your teeth—
filthy fossilized turnips,
canvas lettuce,
concrete carrots
leaving a flinty taste in your mouth.

The teacher is a strict sonneteer
slotting his students' unwieldy syllables
into place, giving them enjambments, iambs, spondees.

He shows you a poem,
pointing to the last two lines:

      "Though the morning was cold, Tom was happy & warm;
      So if all do their duty, they need not fear harm."

The teacher's cleanshaven lips crisply emit the words.

      "Go ahead."

"Thoo the moaning"

The teacher's hand chops the air.

"Though. Though the morning."

You make a fist
& look at your classmates;
your hands are bound & gagged.

"Thuugh"

      "Good."

"Though the moaning"

      "Morning. Mor. Mor-ning."

"Moaning"

"You're not saying the R sound. Ar. Ar. Arrrr."

You smile at the teacher's teeth,
make the sign for "Funny."
The teacher slaps your hand
& you drop the poem. The teacher points
& tells you to sit down.

At night, in the dark, in the quiet,
you carefully fold down your sheet
& sign to the ceiling. An invisible radius
encircles your hands, stifling your movements.
You sign in quick tight motions, whisper your signs.

don't care
poetry go hell
go hell teacher
hate you teacher
stupid bastard

You look around the dorm, hoping to
find someone to share your signs with. You fall
asleep dreading the bucket of cold water.

As the weeks drain away, your signs become
marginal, little finger flicks to fill the silent gaps.

*

"Their voices clatter harshly. Ugly, deformed
voices. No accent: the raw material
from which an accent, a voice, might be formed.
A harsh bark, or an odd ethereal
effect, like the hiccup of a lost soul.
And their diction. The phrases they use.
Embarrassing. They tumble instead of roll
off the tongue. 'Underibewatewy.' Obtuse.
You'd think they're totally illiterate.
They always forget whatever came before.
'Again. Again!' Their mouths goad, irritate.
But then, isn't that what we're paid for,
to teach the kids grammar and poetry
and rectify their verbal poverty?"

*

One night before bed, before the house parent
arrives, you & your dorm mates make
handshapes on the wall.

The others make rabbits & geese;

you make a gorilla, a reindeer &, with
the help of a headless stuffed elephant, a lion,
using the stuffing as a snarled mane,
its grizzled snout nearly lifelike in shadow.

lion pig rat monster

teacher goblin

house parent dick bastard

fuck him

You don't stop,
you can't stop laughing—

your retracted laughter,
your leashed laughter has
like a starved bat left dents
in the walls of your mouth.

*

The church is full of mottled light.
You finger a chip in the pew,
watch the tall priest,
read his lips as best you can,
adjust your clunky hearing aid.
It's like trying to trap echoes in a box.

The priest waves his hands but doesn't sign;
thankfully he has a mouth like a whale shark.

"St. Francis de Sales, the patron saint of the deaf, was born in 1567. One day St.
Francis's servant introduced him to a young deaf man named Martin. Back then,
people thought the deaf were mentally ill. But St. Francis saw that Martin was quite
intelligent, so he took it upon himself to educate him."

The priest beams but doesn't say
how St. Francis educated the deaf man,
leaving you to imagine
     ropes
     cold water
     raw red hands
     speaking exercises that loosened Martin's teeth.

You wonder why the patron saint of the deaf isn't deaf,
wonder if there are any deaf saints,
if a deaf person can achieve sainthood,
if a deaf person can properly receive the word of God.

At night, you decide to become a saint.

At night, beneath the sheets, within the ropes
forming in your mind, you whisper with your hands.

Pamela Mordecai

Pamela Mordecai writes poetry and fiction for children and adults. Her first collection of short stories, *PINK ICING*, appeared in 2006 to enthusiastic reviews. In 2015, her debut novel, *RED JACKET* was shortlisted for the Rogers Writers' Trust Fiction Award. She and her husband, Martin, live in Kitchener, Ontario.

Excerpts from *The Tear Well*

Papa is a serious man. Also Papa is a man of action.

I hear him tell Mama so, time and time again.

"I am a man of action, Nettie. I do what I have to do, and waste no time. It make no sense to waste time, for you well know that some things book no dallying. A person must act with speed, specially when he is bliged to do a difficult thing."

Uncle Percy come to see Papa at our house the same day the ambulance come for Mama. It is a dark day. From morning, clouds piling up thick over the hills and then pushing out over the sky, dropping way down low like a pregnant lady with full big breasts and a fat baby that ready but can't make up its mind to drop. Is well past lunchtime when ambulance arrive and two giant, broad-back people dress in white come inside and take Mama away. That is maybe one hour ago, maybe two or three, for is hard to tell time when a body is crying and crying.

Carole and Petal and Pauline still at school when Uncle Percy ride up on his Lulu motorbike. He speed up the little slope to the space where a decent gate should be and bump in, *brrrm-brrrm*, drag his boots on the ground to slow Lulu down, *scrrrr-scrrrr*, then turn off the bike so sudden it tremble and cough before it stop.

Then he pitch Lulu down, just so, on the ground.

Same time I know something is wrong, for that is not Uncle Percy usual way. No sir. He always slide in on a pretty turn, dolly round on Lulu in a big circle, then slip around easy on a smaller circle, as he take time to slow down and stop, hold Lulu still as he swing over his foot and leap right off, smooth and show-offy as you please. Uncle Percy love that Lulu bike, always treat her like a high class lady, polish and shine her with his bright yellow chamois cloth, stand her up with the silver stick like a magic wand, pat Lulu on her seat, tell her, "Thanks, Lulu girl, for bringing me safe!"

Lulu is Uncle Percy faithful friend.

I am hiding in the bed of hibiscus on Miss Clooney side of the house when Uncle Percy roll up on Lulu. The hibiscus bushes go all the way down on the two sides of the house. They start where the open verandah stop and the house it very self begin, and go on down beside the long thin house to right at the end, where the kitchen is.

As soon as I see Mama step in the ambulance van, the stone in my chest break up in little pieces. From that time till now I am bawling living eye-water. Can't stop, don't mind how I try. I don't know who I most vex with. With Papa for letting the two gorilla people take Mama away, or with the gorilla people their very selves, or with me myself, for it is all sake of me. If I never fall down, none of this would happen.

But what am I to do?

If I was not all alone, maybe it would be better. If I had Carole or Pauline, even Petal for company, somebody to say, "Never mind, Rubes — is so life go," or "Hush, Rubes, hush, it will pass in time," maybe I wouldn't cry so much. But is just me alone, me and Papa. And Papa don't like when anybody cry. Only time we must cry is when he beat us; any other time and he get mad like wasp when you trouble their nest.

That don't stop me crying, for some things don't book no choice, like him, Papa, say when he ready. Still, I not looking for trouble on this day, for it well full up of trouble already. After Mama gone, I come outside because I know if Papa hear me inside crying, he will rap his belt buckle with his first finger, frown-up his forehead and warn me, in his soft-soft voice, "Listen, Ruby. If you don't stop that cow-bawling, I will be bliged to give you something you can really cry about!"

Papa is wrong. Don't care if he is old as Mefuselah in the Bible and strong like Sampson, who is in the Bible too. Don't care if he is my father. If Mama is gone away, that is worth plenty crying for.

From I come here and stand up, I wipe my eyes and nose with my skirt so much times that it is all wet with eye-water and nose-nought. I know if Papa see me, is plenty shouting bout how I make a mess of my clothes. Carole not going like it neither, for like how Mama gone, is she going to deal with Miss Joy, see to cooking and cleaning, make sure everybody have clothes for school and work and church, doing the things Mama is usual to do as best as only a young girl, can.

Can't worry bout that now, though, for I feel weak like a just-born baby puss. All the wetness gone out of my body, and there is no more water left in the tear well that my two eye draw from. One thing I can say for certain: when a person is done crying out all their eye-water, that is a plenty worse feeling than when they are crying and crying. That time your insides is all dry and dusty, choke-up and strangle-out of every last thing, wetness and air, laughing and talking, smelling and tasting and touching and all. I not even sure I am here in this world any more for it feel like all the stuffing that make me firm and solid is gone right out of me.

"You see, it all adds up, my Ruby!" That is Mama. She teach me that water make up most of our body. But is me, all by myself figure out that if a person cry out all their wetness, then most of that person must be gone with the water. Maybe it work in the same way as when you sigh and sigh until you sigh out your blood.

Papa is waiting to talk to Uncle Percy on the smooth green concrete verandah that Mama polish and shine with the coconut brush Wednesday and Saturday, knocking Johnny Cooper music, karup-kup-kup, karup-kup-kup, to make us laugh, letting us try after we beg her, "Please, please, Mama, pleeeease! Can we knock Johnny Cooper too?"

My crying place where I am hiding is at the corner of the verandah on the other side from where Papa with his stiff neck is waiting and watching as Uncle Percy cover the short distance from where he leave his Lulu bike with a few big steps. Papa stand up like a spotty red bug with a round head sprinkle with dry orange hairs in the flowers and plants Mama put on the verandah, pots with pink and red anthurirums and every colour of bug-in-a-villa, and my favourites, caladimums that Miss Joy call Angel Wings.

I turn my head and see big fat Miss Clooney hiding too, pulling back the lace curtain at her window and peeping across in her green muu-muu. She drop the curtain and look away when she see me turn my head, but I know that dance from long ago, like Mama say, "Go ahead. Snoop and sniff, Miss Eleanor, then make comments to Miss Minna longside."

I hear Uncle Percy ride up on the bike and I think he come so Papa can tell him what happen to Mama. That time I decide to stay and listen. I think, it don't matter if they take her and fly her to the moon, I need to know where Mama is, and if I can see her, and if she is going to come home soon like she promise. But when Uncle Percy stop his Lulu bike, bup, and throw it down on the grass just so, I get worried and I think he see Mama already and he now come with news about Mama and is not good news. Maybe he in a hurry to tell Papa and never mind he love the Lulu bike, he love his sister Nettie plenty more, so that's why he just throw down the Lulu bike, rushing up to give his information to Papa

When I see him step to the verandah in big long, thumping steps, that time my body come all over with shivers and chicken-skin bumps. I can see from the crunch of his jaw and the shub-out of his bottom lip that nothing good going come out of this visit with Papa, for I know how it look when a cock is fixing to fight a next cock.

Uncle Percy hop up the three steps and stand up square in front of Papa, like they are going to wrestle or play pat-a-cake. Papa is shorter than Uncle Percy, but he is thick, and now he lean out his solid chest like a bantam rooster. Uncle Percy pull up himself to his tallest tall and gaze down on Papa like a mighty Jesus from his throne on high. Only difference is he have a terrible look on his face. I don't think Jesus face would ever sport a look like that.

Uncle Percy make as if to say something, but Papa jump in first before any sound can finish making its way out the O of Uncle Percy mouth.

"I had no alternative, Percy. The situation was deadly serious. The police were here. I did what I thought it best to do and I immediately left messages for you and Max, as we agreed. You cannot possibly be annoyed."

Uncle Percy don't say anything, just snarl *rowr, rowr,* and drag his lips back over his teeth like a bad dog when it getting ready to bite.

I know Uncle Percy love Mama bad. Uncle Percy come first in Mama family. Uncle Max come next, then Mama at the end like me. And Mama is special because she is the one girl.

Uncle Percy is tall and slender. He is strong and black as the ace of spades. I know about the ace of spades, which is mightiest ace in the pack, because if Papa not coming home for dinner, Mama and me play cards right when we finish lunch. If Papa not coming, tea is plentiful and dinner is light.

Papa don't like cards for is a "game of chance". Mama tired to remind him, "Evan. Life itself is a game of chance!"

From where I am hiding, through the shiny dark green hearts of the hibiscus leaves I can see Uncle Percy face. I can't see Papa face, for his back is to me, but I can see Uncle Percy face very plain, especially one side of it, for the light of the sun that is getting low in the sky is falling in a glow right there. Boy, oh boy! Uncle Percy don't only sound like a rabid dog, he look like one too. I think if he was ever to sink his two eye-teeth into Papa, Papa bound to get lockjaw and fall down dead! He look like all the power in his body gather up in his face which is turning purple, like a garden egg filling out on the bush of his body, getting riper and riper, darker and darker as I watch.

 "Evan Dalhousie, seems to me you must be gone right straight off your head. You think you can shove and push my sister, haul and pull her, fling her in the pound as though she is a stray dog that you scrape up off of some stinking street corner?"

"Let the cord show that is you who furred to Nettie as a stray dog. No such words came out of my mouth."

"That is a perfect example of how your screaming mind work. I say you cannot shove and push my sister *as though* she is a stray dog. As though! As though! If you speak Queen English, you know 'as though'!"

"I hear exactly what you are saying, Percy, including 'as though'. But Nettie is my wife and so I have to deal with her cording as I think best, especially in her current sick state, if neither you nor Max can be reached right off. "

Sick! Papa say Mama is sick! But Mama is not sick. Mama is well, as well as always. Make the beds, clean the house, darn little holes and big holes, sew dress and blouse and uniform, cook every single day, write up the laundry book with the clothes Miss Joy is to wash and iron when she come on Tuesday morning. No sir. Plenty people sick, yes, but Mama not sick. Is true she take a little cry sometimes, but mostly she smile soft as the fuzz on baby chicks. And every time after she cry, she sniff and blow her nose, and then she is ready to go again. No sir. Papa is wrong. Mama is not sick.

"I warn you, Evan, I am not putting up with it. Max is not putting up with it neither. So take careful note. Read my moving mouth. We will not dure it, not from the Queen of England and not from a bucket of X-cement like you!"

X-cement? X-cement? Papa is a bucket of X-cement?

Uncle Percy voice is soft but rumbling, not like a dog anymore but like a lion trying to cough up something that stick deep down in his throat.

"Percival Fenton, get off my property."

"Your property! This is now your property? You tiefing, low-down, yellow snake." Mama teach me that the yellow snake is not poisonous. It has a small pointed head and lives in cool distant places. It feeds on birds and rats and bats and some kinds of eggs. I don't like snake and lizard even though Mama say they are God's creatures and harmless, for they don't trouble you unless you trouble them. But when Uncle Percy say Papa is a yellow snake, I don't think he mean that Papa is harmless. So maybe somebody trouble Papa and make him into a harmful snake. I don't know who to ask about that, though. Is only Mama I could ask and Mama is not here.

Uncle Percy clearing his throat deeper and deeper. Then I see his mouth and his throat start to work as he hawk and gather up the nastiness from way deep down in his chest. Oh Jesus, Mary and Joseph! Uncle Percy is going to spit in Papa face! But no. He swallow it down, turn away, stamp so hard down the steps of the verandah that the roof and the posts all shiver and shake. He march over to where Lulu bike is on the grass. He lift her with one arm, throw his foot over, settle down on her seat. Then he turn and look at Papa. When he speak, it is one word at a time, like Mama when she dealing cards.

"Evan. Dalhousie. I. Swear. To. God. That. Max. And. Me. Going. Fix. Your. Rass!"

Uh-oh! Papa is not going to stand for that. There is to be no swearing or foul language in these premises! Sometimes shit jump out of Mama mouth. Any time that happen, she make like a zip across her lip. She squeeze her lips together like in a kiss, put her finger in front of them, and tell me, in a whisper, "Rubes, remember! You never heard me say that!" I smile and nod my head to tell her I understand. Not a chance I am going to say anything to get Mama in trouble. Better I die, dead as a Sunday dinner fowl.

Uncle Percy not finished talking. He roll the bike right up to the verandah where Papa is standing. His face now look crumpled up, broken and sad, like Humpty Dumpty would look if a doctor manage to sew all the pieces together after he drop off the wall. His voice is very low. It is his duppy voice, and it frighten me worse than when he was growling.

"If our sister suffer the smallest injury at your hands, Dalhousie, you whited sepicur, you wolf in sheep clothing, I promise you sonemly, you will not live to tell the tale."

Then Uncle Percy kick-start his Lulu bike and roar up to the gate space, bump over it and roar out, zoom-zooming off with his mash-up-and-stitch-up, pur- ple-garden-egg face.

And same time like a big breeze pick up the leaves and branches and dirt and dust and bubble gum wrappers and bits of fudge sticks in the street in front of our house and twist them round and round. They rise in a spinning tunnel from the ground to the sky that put me in mind of Dorothy and Toto and the big tornado and the yellow brick road. And like in a vision, I see a hissing yellow snake sliding across the road. I never see nothing like that twisting, curling air before. I am so surprised I nearly run out of my hiding place to see it better.

"Black bastard!" I hear Papa say, clear as day. "Bloody, low class, criminal of a black bastard."

I can't believe is Papa using language like that! Is the kind of words that he beat us for. If we say any word like that, first he wash out our mouth with carbolic soap, and then, if is not a very bad word, we get the cane in our hand middle and if is a bad-bad word, we get licks on our bottom! But I know it must be Papa using that terrible language, for nobody is left here now — not a soul but him and me.

I don't wait to see Papa face when he turn around to go back in the house. I take time and go back, tipping on my toes. One step. Two step. Three, four, five. Then I turn and run fast as a mongoose to the back of the house. I scoop up some corn from the bin near the kitchen door. I run quick-quick to the gate of the fowl coop. Open the gate and step right in. Start to throw corn, right and left, far and near, spinning in a circle, drizzling out corn.

If Papa find me in here, I will say the hens look hungry and I am tending to them, chucking them corn, and changing their water, and then after that I am going to search for eggs.

"I know it is getting late, Papa," I will say, "but when they start good laying, is morning and evening we feed them and is morning and evening we search."

Papa will never know if is foolishness I am telling him.

Papa never, never go in that fowl coop.

Papa don't like things that fly at him all of a sudden.

Papa don't like fowl doo-doo on his clothes.

Papa don't like how the fowl coop stink.

Is only ever Mama and me.

And now Mama is gone, is only me to tend to our chicken family.

SENNAH YEE

Sennah Yee

Sennah Yee is from Toronto, where she writes poetry, writes about films, and writes poetry about films. She is the author of the poetry/non-fiction book *HOW DO I LOOK?* (Metatron Press, 2017). She has a MA in Cinema & Media Studies and focused her research on gendered robot design. www.sennahyee.com

5 Haiku for/from Canada

I
ask me where I'm from
and I'll just say the same thing
o, Canada, duh

II
you're frightened that I've
flourished right in the hyphen
that you've slapped on me

III
"we're more polite here!"
so polite we say nothing
and smile about it

IV
us vs. JT:
disappointed not surprised
sorry not sorry

V
you tell me "go home!"
we both go our own way
you order Chinese

Blade Runner 2049 (2017)

I can be whatever you want me to be—except flesh and bone. Is a body not enough if it cannot touch or be touched? Can you love me without touching me? Can you touch me without loving me? Would you like me to tell you the truth or a lie? Here are some: You are special. I am special. You are free to go wherever you'd like. You are free to go. You are free.

多倫多華埠

When I get my hair cut in Chinatown, I think of how there must be a very long word to describe the specific joy and sadness I feel here, where everyone looks like me, where no one looks at me, where I do not know how to tell anyone how happy this makes me. Perhaps this very long word exists in Chinese—I would not know.

But I'm A Cheerleader (2000)

We watch it every single year in my high school's GSA. When Clea DuVall reaches out and touches Natasha Lyonne's arm in the dark, I watch you watch me pretending to watch the scene from the corners of my eyes. I am thinking of the back of your ears, the creases on the inside of your elbow, the hair on your knuckles. I am thinking of us, apart, together.

Wanderlust

I have traveled halfway across the world

to have white backpackers make me feel alien

in the very continent that they insist I am "really" from

Micro

Fourth grade lunch. Noisy cafeteria. I'm eating a sandwich cut into squares instead of triangles, because dad made it that day instead of mum. You're sitting across from me, chewing with your mouth open. You ask me to help translate a phrase from a *Digimon* episode.

I don't know what you mean—but I clarify that *Pokémon's* superior. Airborne crumbs as you exclaim a string of foreign words and then look at me expectantly. I blink back.

"I still don't know what that means."

Disappointment on your chewy face. "Oh. I just thought you'd know 'cause you're Chinese... right?"

I pause and then nod. Right. "Isn't *Digimon* Japanese, though?"

Pause. You move onto slurping loudly from your juicebox.

"I dunno. Whatever."

I leave my crusts behind, brush your crumbs off the table.

*

We're in your bedroom, listening to the *Garden State* movie soundtrack. You're helping me put on makeup for the very first time. You have a YouTube eyeliner tutorial open on your computer that you keep pausing and replaying as your hand trembles on my eyelid, sometimes grazing my cheek. I'm trying to keep my eyes open and still, but I don't know where to look.

You sigh, lower your hand.

"What's wrong?"
You cap your eyeliner, exit YouTube, log onto Facebook.

"Sorry, I can' t do it," you mutter. "It's too hard to do with your eye shape."

"Can I see in the mirror, anyway?"

"No, don't."

*

Outdoor Frosh Week dance. Mediocre top 40s pop earwig of the hour. Not enough space to put our hands up in the air as the song tells us to. A lot of girls have snipped up their oversized frosh shirts to look sexy. Now I regret being too lazy to unpack my things in my dorm earlier. Things like scissors. I feebly try to bunch up my T-shirt and knot it off to the side. You can kind of see my hipbone, maybe, sort of. I try to put my hands up in the air. I elbow someone's head next to me, but my hipbone's showing. That'll do.

Enter you dancing next to me. I'm endeared by your blond hair, and how I can see all your freckles even in the dark. We go through the usual questions of the week, and their usual answers: name, major, hometown, and a quip about the shit music they're playing or something to round the whole intro off. You're cynical but not a know-it-all. You play guitar and want to master drums. You stay for the credits of the movie. We're hitting it off.

Then you tell me that my English is really good.

"What?!" I shout, partially because we're right by the blaring speakers, but mostly because I can't believe my ears—or what's left of them.

"I said *your English is really good!*" you shout back, with a big thumbs-up.

I stare, petrified. Then I dance my way outta there.

*

You walk into the not-really-fast food restaurant I work at. You're old, ele-phant-skinned, wearing a generic baseball cap and a neon windbreaker that I can only assume you've kept from your 80s prime. You place your order and talk to me as you wait. The usual. *It's getting darker earlier now. At least Christmas is soon. I like the music you're playing here. Can I guess your back-ground?*

My toothy customer service smile flickers at the last one.

"Hm... Japanese...?" you ask, even though I never answered your initial question.

"No, Canadian."

"But your paren—"

"Born in Toronto, too."

"And your grandparents?"

"From China."

Finally, I've said the magic word.

"Ah! Yes, I just thought I'd ask, since you have Oriental features."

I'm a pack of noodles, a porcelain doll. You're still smiling warmly at me, and it almost makes it worse that I know you mean no harm. Order up—you thank me for helping pass the time.

"You're welcome," I say, toothy customer service smile switched back on. "*Domo arigato*," you reply, before leaving with your burger. The door swings shut.

*

Summertime, FIFA World Cup 2014. My family and I have been diehard fans of the German National Team since 2006. During the final match between Germany and Argentina, my family and I are decked out in German soccer jerseys, flowery leis, and huge flags draped on our shoulders. We're curled up on our living room couch in fetal position as our beloved team goes into overtime.

When Mario Götze scores the winning goal, we hop around, crying out of delight and relief that it's finally over, and we *won*.

My older sister and I scramble outside to walk along Bloor Street and celebrate. We get happy honks here and there from cars passing by, German flags fluttering from their windows.

From a bench you spot us on the sidewalk and smile, somewhat amused.

"Congratulations!"

"Thanks!" My sister and I reply brightly, waving our flags around. My face hurts from smiling so much.

That air of amusement's still on your face, and mine and my sisters' smiles start fading. You're staring at us now.

"Why Germany...?" you finally say. "What's your affiliation with it?"

"We just love the team," we say. Would you ever ask a white guy with zero Italian in him why he's rooting for team Italy?

You raise an eyebrow, nod. "Alright, then!"

The sun scorches our black hair and makes us squint our eyes even smaller. We tuck our hair under baseball caps and put on our sunglasses. We march on.

K
A
I
E

K
E
L
L
O
U
G
H

Kaie Kellough

Kale Kellough is a novelist, poet, and sound performer. He is the author of the novel *Accordéon*, which was a finalist for the Amazon First Novel Award. His latest work is *Magnetic Equator* (poetry, McClelland and Stewart, 2019). His upcoming collection of short stories, *Dominoes at the Crossroads*, will appear in 2020 with Véhicule Press.

Capital

It was twilight in the permanent collection. Each painting was accompanied by a caption and a date that reached far back into the colonial period. We emerged squinting into the morning brilliance flooding the gallery. We leaned on the railing and looked down to the main floor, its massive gray tiles, and out the grid of windows that reached to the roof. We stared over the frozen canal, the denuded trees pale in the winter sun. The houses of Parliament rose atop a hill in the distance. Their weathered stone and the patina of their copper roofs seemed permanent, as if the present itself were a colonial painting composed in 1759.

I leaned on the railing next to Angélique. She withdrew her arm, but I leaned into the tension, thinking about *The Death of General Wolfe*, about the triangulated focus of the painting, how it guided the viewer's gaze past Wolfe collapsed like a messiah in the arms of his doctors and generals, and up to the British flag, bunched and fallen, in the arms of a soldier. These two sentimental embraces, of the flag of empire and its sacrificed soldier, mirror one another. Somehow, though, the painting succeeds in spite of this extravagance. If we remove all of its ornaments, it narrates the death of a man important to others, and those others are gathered around him in various attitudes of anxiety, dejection, despair. We believe their expressions. The cooler gray heads of the doctor and the senior generals seem to know that Wolfe will die, with bullets that have torn through his red coat and pierced his torso, and they only seem intent on comforting him in his last moments. The others, the wounded, dizzied soldiers at a loss for direction, steady themselves against their fellows as they look on in anguish and disbelief.

Great columns of smoke rise in the distance and darken the corner of the painting that hangs above the dying general. A messenger rushes up, but Wolfe is about to expire, and the messenger is forever frozen in his urgent approach. He never arrives. He bears the message that the French surrendered after only six—or sixteen—minutes of battle, that General Montcalm was shot in the stomach, and that in spite of all of the turmoil, the British empire will raise its flag over the *Plaines d'Abraham* again.

The most compelling character in the painting is the Indigenous warrior in the foreground, conspicuously kneeling in the pose of of Rodin's *Thinker*, staring at General Wolfe. His mouth is open, tucked down at its corners, and his expression is ambiguous. He is clearly moved. By turns he looks concerned, as anyone would be at the violent death of another human being, but there is some confusion in his look. The messenger hasn't yet reached with his news, and in the frozen imminence of the painting, he never will. Maybe the confusion arises because he doesn't feel anything. Maybe he realizes that, as Gwendolyn Brooks later wrote, "Nobody loves a master." He also looks like he's about to speak, to pronounce something, but will he speak to himself, will he address everyone gathered at Wolfe's side, or will he speak straight to the dying general, perhaps offering a prayer to speed Wolfe to the afterlife, or a curse? Or maybe he'll suddenly turn to face the person viewing the painting and will say, "Make sure that this painting stays in the basement of the National Gallery forever, and that all of the Indigenous art is housed on the top floor," and maybe I am the only one who hears this commentary. I then wonder whether he's laughing, laughing at the melodrama of the scene, at the romantic colonial ambitions of the painter, at the way in which General Wolfe seems to be swooning like a lover spurned.

And then we were out of the permanent collection. I turned to Angélique and said, "The Indigenous art should not be in the fucking basement, across from the washrooms, while the colonial art is up here on the second floor."

Angélique measured her tone: "Suppose we did make that switch, then what would we move to the basement? Would we move The Group of Seven?"

"Yes. Stash them in the basement."

Angélique snickered. "Or the colonial painters like Joseph Légaré and Benjamin West? This is the National Gallery of Canada. Its sole purpose is to tell the story of *Canada*, not to advocate for social justice."

"But some of those colonial painters weren't even Canadian. They were Irish, British, French. And plus, Canada didn't even exist back then, it was just a colony, so we can take some narrative liberties with their inclusion and their status. Their paintings can hang right across from the washrooms."

"This conversation is too obvious."

"Obvious?"

"Just write your Twitter essay and scrap it out there, but not with me."

"What is your point? I was just enjoying the exhibit. Sure it has its problems, but do we have to politicize every fucking thing?"

"Everything is politicized. Plus, I grew up in Toronto, where the Group of Seven was lorded over us like the arrival point of all culture, to the exclusion of everyone else. If that isn't political..."

"Sure, okay, okay, okay, fine. You can have your politics, but let me have my uninterrupted thoughts about the exhibit. You don't have to assault and subvert everything."

"You're wrong. I do have to critique and subvert everything, and I will. That's the point."

"Don't do it in my ear." Angélique turned back into the exhibit. I stood on the landing and stared toward our painted Parliament.

*

I was in Québec city playing a jazz series. After the show we sat around drinking, and one of the musicians, a contrebasse player who grew up in Québec, displayed this wild, unusual laugh. It was the classic laugh of a Marvel villain, a sonorous Mwa-ha-ha-ha-ha that started out in the mid-register, then deepened and resonated as his mouth opened wider and wider. People at other tables glanced over their shoulders each time he laughed. After several rounds and I don't remember how many dips outside to smoke, one of the musicians asked him where the laugh came from.

He let out the loudest laugh of the evening, one that interrupted the conversations at neighboring tables, then he grinned, "I got it on July 11th, 2004."

Kaie Kellough   051

Someone else asked, "You remember the exact date? How is that possible? A laugh doesn't have a date of birth. Are you serious?"

"Oh yeah, I'm serious." He grinned. "Does anyone remember what happened on July 11th, 2004?"

Nobody offered any ideas. He hinted, "It was on the Plains of Abraham." We shook our heads.

"As I said, it was on the Plains of Abraham. It was during the F*estival d'Été du Québec*, and it was raining nonstop. The festival headliner was the French punk band Bérurier Noir, and fifty thousand people showed up for the concert. The entire plains was churned into mud. People were covered in mud. Apparently the stage had to be squeegeed before the performance because so much water gathered on it. At one point I swear I saw the stage crackle blue with electricity."

"At the time I played in a band called *Bomb la Bourse*," he snickered, "and my ambition was to gig in Montréal." He lifted up his shirt and exposed his skinny brown flank, where the flesh was raised into an A with a circle around it. He grinned as he dropped his shirt.

"I got high and then got separated from my friends at the concert, and there were so many people, it was getting dark, I couldn't find my way back so I just wandered. I got soaked and took in all the people. It was overwhelming, exciting, like…" He went quiet and glanced down. We watched his face.

"Imagine that on the Plains, every subculture of Québec punk was represented, from the street squeegees to—I didn't know this at the time—several different groups of Fachos, who—"

"What's a Facho?"

"A Fascist, a Nazi. Some of them were up from Montréal. They had been planning for the event for months, and their purpose was to disrupt the concert and rumble. I had no idea about this, and I unknowingly wandered into their camp. All I remember is being soaked through, and looking around at the punks, but not really at anyone in particular, just taking in the vastness of the wet, muddy scene. It was incredible, and suddenly a couple of big *Québs* were shoving me around and yelling at me: "Qu'es-ce-tu fais icitte toé? Qu'es-ce-tu fais icitte LeBrun?" They smelled like beer. Others were laughing, and some drunk chick said: "Hey just leave 'im alone...*hostie* d'fuckin' skinny Paki, go back where 'e come from," and there was more laughter, then someone was pouring beer over my head, and then there was a massive commotion. Someone else grabbed me, people were shouting, then punches were being thrown, and I was being shoved in some direction, and there was a lot of shouting and surging, as if the Plains themselves tilted and everyone lost their balance, but it wasn't that. It was some Antifa from Montréal—"

"What's Antifa?"

"Anti Fascists. SHARPs. Skinheads Against Racial Prejudice. Yeah, some big Antifa dudes from Hochelag, Pointe-Ste-Charles, Verdun, they'd heard about what the Fachos were planning and decided to confront them on the Plains, and there

I was, a totally stoned, oblivious brown dude who wandered through the middle of it and set off a white race riot. I don't know what happened after that though, because I got jostled around and then I popped out the other end of the rumble. I was standing by a group of stoned punks who were from Montréal as well, and who offered me a beer and a smoke and said: "You look like you need it, man." So I took the beer, and I shared a joint with them, and..." The bassist stared into his lap.

He looked back up. "And then I remember feeling like...like...you're gonna think I'm crazy, but I guess I am, so: I felt like I had a trillion ultra-ultra-slim acupuncture needles covering my cranium. The needles felt good, and they reached up into the air, miles and miles above the clouds, and out through the hole in the ozone layer. As the earth rotated, the needles swayed in one direction and then another, tickling my cranium. It felt incredible, like my head was somehow plugged into the cosmos and was receiving electric impulses from somewhere beyond the stratosphere.

"And then I kind-of came to my senses a couple of days later, standing outside a metro station shouting at a public telephone. I was eventually picked up, and hospitalized, and medicated. My parents brought me home, and ever since then I've had that laugh. The only thing is, I don't know where I went over those two days, how I got from the concert in Québec into downtown Montréal, or anything that happened to me. I've always wondered whether I'll ever remember, whether I want to remember." He grinned and let out a sonorous laugh, but everyone else stayed quiet.

"When my parents finally took me home, my dad thought I needed healing music, so he played Alice Coltrane records over and over: *Journey In Satchidananda, Ptah the El Daoud, Universal Consciousness, Eternity, World Galaxy.* I realized that the music was delivering a message to me alone. Only I could decode it. The message was that I would understand the message only if I devoted my life to music that communicated peaceably with all living things, as an antidote to the rage and consternation of the world."

*

I turned away from the view of the frozen canal, of Parliament Hill rising in the distance, the age of its buildings comforting yet disturbingly permanent. I felt an ache for my horn, a desire for its sound to emerge as loud as it would from the speakers on the *Plaines d'Abraham.* I wanted to stand on the mezzanine and play—not a melody, but a stream of expletive notes, ones that would crack the stones of parliament, sunder the foundations from the earth. Maybe the buildings would tremble, lean, and in a blurred streak of color, slide into the canal.

I stayed on the mezzanine, contemplating how the rupture of one world is echoed in the next. Angélique had left me. She had slipped back into the permanent collection. I knew she was examining *The Death of General Wolfe.* She could sit there for as long as she needed, trying to identify something of herself, something of her world in the immobile drama of that canvas.

Charlie Petch

Charlie Petch is an award winning playwright, musician, lighting designer and spoken word artist. They tour internationally as a feature and also their spoken word theatre shows, *"Mel Malarkey Gets the Bum's Rush"* and *"Daughter Of Geppetto"*. They are a member of the League of Canadian Poets and have been published by *Descant, The Malahat, Matrix* and more. *Lyrical Myrical* published *"Late Night Knife Fights"* their first collection. Find out more at www.charliecpetch.com or @sawpoet.

My First Boyfriend

Before you killed someone,
I watched you pull my drunk friend out of the water
and breathe mist on a dock.
I handed you my sweater,
watched you pull your shirt over your head,
lights lapping at lake water chest.

Before you killed someone,
your mouth full of shy,
you gave me a beaded bracelet,
that was so mismatched,
I knew your sister didn't help.

Before you killed someone,
we were barefoot,
callused with summer.
You held sumac to my face,
inhaled its iced tea fragrance.

Before you killed someone,
I sat in your room,
played the game we had as children,
tortured Ethel the action figure.
your little brother came in

dropped the key out of his
grenade mouth.
Two feet taller than him
you appeared one inch tall,
by the time I stopped laughing,
to look.

Before you killed someone,
I listened to kids who told me
you were a loser,
friends I never had before,
ones I secretly wanted,
cracked your twelve-year-old heart.
Put the bracelet into your hand,
the one I used to hold.

Years later, your parents left too.
Sent you to military school.
Not everyone can raise the children they get

I went to your birthday party,
ended up hiding in a washroom,
for fear of military boys,
who grab your chest,
hold you like weaponry.

My first boyfriend was lost to be found,
accepted payment to kill a stranger,
a wife cloying with sumac breath,
your chance to be bully,
you bragged about it to a girl,
who was so impressed she called the cops.

Before you killed that man,
maybe the world felt like prison.
Every escape attempt
another clanging door.
Girl's laughter like lockdown

I remember the boy you might have been
smell sumac carefully.
Did you know it was poison then?
That enemies can smell sweet?
That betrayal is part of growing up?
That my first boyfriend
started off heroic?

Daughter of Geppetto

When the woodsman
handed me to you Geppetto,
when I was
a mere talking log
and only knew one thing
to tell my creator
that
"I'm to be a real boy."
Though you heard me,
you flexed your jaw
and whittled me
into your wish
for a daughter
named "Pinocchia."

Father isn't life a
funny tide?
When I was washed
into the belly of a shark,
one so big it swallowed your ship,
I found you
eating the fish
that clapped at your feet,
you grinned a shine of scales

and cried out
"Pinocchia!"

I should have been full of mirth,
for I thought you dead for years,
but what came out of my mouth was:

"No father
It's me,
your son
Pinocchio"

and I waited for that old rage,
the one that called me sick,
called me devil,
called me daughter,
that shouted me from our little hut,

but you smiled,
as if you had to make room
for six rows of teeth.
Greeted me "Pinocchio"
and it was then
I saw
what living so long in
the belly of a shark

can do to a person.

Father Geppetto
you suffer a softened mind,
remember little,
and can be convinced
of anything.

This is our true story

Sometimes father,
back when I slept
at your feet,
I would beg the Faerie
to change me into
a soft thing.
Something to never be named,
only loved and held like
your blanket,
your pillow .

Father I'm sorry
that after I left
you became
the town spectare.
A wearied violence.

A voice
that slapped
the sides of houses,
demanding your daughter
"Pinocchia" be returned.

You should
have looked for me
instead.
I told you my name
before I left.

Today,
as I cut your nails,
you asked me
if we could read later.
Had I written another chapter
in our book,
"The Adventures
of Pinocchio",
how was it coming?

Father, I write it only
when you are
asleep.
I walk out into the woods,

so as to not
shatter the windows
with the menace of
birds that arrive.
Their wings a circus tent
that ink out the sky,
their beaks thirsty
to erase this lie of a nose,
that winds and curls,
as I create the story
I want you to hear.

What a deep vertigo
you are in Father
and I'm ashamed
that it brings me peace
to never hear
you call me
Pinocchia again.

And Father thank you,
I hear your prayers
each night,
asking the faerie
turn me into
a real boy

before you die.

But that old wish
means nothing
to me.

Yesterday
you held me and said,
"Pinocchio you
are such a fine son
such a good lad."

Father this is
all I've ever needed
is to feel real
in your eyes.

My name is Pinocchio
and this is my true story.

Speaking Bradbury

Time held us
between sheets,
by the lamplight,
our anatomy easy
and in love.

I opened the covers
of Ray Bradbury,
used his words to
paint orbits around your head,
swing us from one tattoo
to the next.
Tracing the body
of the Illustrated Woman.

You'd always fall asleep,
though I'm a good storyteller
(I've been told by myself),
but nothing else in life
would let you abandon
consciousness
with such ease.

Though your sister held your hand
as you died

and our wedding ring
has been buried in the backyard
since before you left
and you hadn't heard my voice in years,

I hope somehow it returned.
Held you past the sundown
that always made you sad,
spoke to you of Mars
melancholy,
and all things fantastic.
That you somehow knew
how loved you always were.

07

Doretta Lau

Doretta Lau is the author of the short story collection *How Does a Single Blade of Grass Thank the Sun?* (Nightwood Editions, 2014). She splits her time between Vancouver and Hong Kong, where she is writing a comic novel about a dysfunctional workplace called *We Are Underlings*.

At Core We Think They Will Kill Us

"Each time it begins in the same way, it doesn't begin the same way, each time it beings it's the same." –Claudia Rankine

I.

When I was in the last year of high school, my family moved into a custom-built house with both a den and a living room on the first floor. Each room had radiant heating—I no longer had to sleep under five blankets because the heater was broken or sit on a freezing cold toilet seat again. I had early acceptance and a full scholarship to the university I'd gone to for free dental care as a child. We'd made it: in a single generation my parents had propelled themselves from post-war poverty to suburban middle class abundance, as evidenced by the three-pack of Pringles from Costco in the pantry, the giant box of Tide in the laundry room, the set of Great Books published by the Encyclopedia Britannica, the shiny black Kawai piano, and the braces on my brother's teeth.

This new home was so much bigger than our previous place that we needed new furniture. My mom and I went to the Bay to buy a couch and love seat. We walked around the showroom floor, dodging some really ugly sofas and then we saw it: a wood-frame couch with upholstery bearing a plaid pattern. It passed the look test, but did it pass the comfort test?

As we were sitting on this sofa that we were sure we were going to buy, laughing in that merry way when you're about to make a big purchase that is a serious life upgrade, a white woman marched over and hissing, "Up, up," while gesturing at us to get up. She did not work for the Bay.

I felt rage burn through me, the kind of rage that is so bright that I feel blind when it sears inside my body. "We are going to buy this," I said.

2.

Events like this play out over and over again. In Hawaii at age thirteen, waiting outside my hotel room door with my mom, a white woman running over to demand the two of us clean her room. At a Richard Serra exhibition, as I jump up in joy over seeing his sculptures in person, a white woman stopping to lecture me about his art practice. "You should really know this history instead of dancing around." As if she was doing me a favour with her condescension. As if I did not already know all about his work. Four a.m. at a McDonald's in New York, a white woman screaming at me about Woody Allen and Soon-Yi Previn, "Go eat at a Chinese restaurant if you want hot food." A literary festival director mocking me for being impressed that a friend's father built a house in Saskatchewan with no previous construction experience, saying, "There is this thing called a library that people visited when they needed to fix something."

Just after the eclipse, I posted about a hostel modeled on cage homes in Hong Kong on Facebook. It cut to the bone because I come from poor people; though I am invited to attend parties at galleries, until quite recently one of my aunts was a cleaner at a museum. I critiqued the hostel's concept—it was clear to me that it was a form of poverty tourism. At no point did I mention the owner (I had no idea it was owned by a person, not a hospitality group).

Yet a white man was quick to jump in and make it personal and question my judgment. "Why do you assume that [redacted] is offering some kind of 'cage home experience'? It has been around for years and its owner [redacted] is very involved in the Sham Shui Po community...I can see why you would see similarities to cage homes, based on the use of wire mesh in the bunk beds. But my real concern is why you seem to think the space is advertising itself as some kind of place where people can 'slum it' with a cage home experience in Sham Shui Po." He tagged the owner to call her attention to my post. It was clear he was out for a fight. Someone else chimed in to defend [redacted], who owns an entire multi-story building in Hong Kong, a city where Forbes reports a square foot of space costs about US$11,000. They insisted that I was wrong, writing that [redacted] did not intend for the hostel to look like cage homes. Take that in: on my short social media post about poverty, two people jumped in to gaslight me about what I was seeing on behalf of their landlord friend.

I could feel Claudia Rankine's words within me as that familiar searing rage began to crawl through my body: "Certain moments send adrenaline to the heart, dry out the tongue, and clog the lungs." People feel free to speak to me like this, like I am a simpleton who requires an education. Like I am not a human being with the full range of emotions. They would never dare to do this if I wasn't an Asian woman. Their subconscious makes them think I am lesser than, even if they believe themselves to be good, anti-racist people. Nice liberals who travel the world and don't see colour, not thinking that willfully ignoring difference is a form of violent erasure.

I've never known what to do when a grown ass man goes full Becky on me, so I thanked everyone for the discussion, deleted the post, and went out to exercise. Even though I was once told that if someone attacks you, one of you is going to end up in the hospital so you better make sure it's not you, I walked away without throwing down. But it wasn't over.

3.

The next day The South China Morning Post ran a story about the hostel. The owner, [redacted], and the designer both talked about how they were inspired by cage homes.

As I processed this information, which proved that my assessment had been correct all along—this wasn't a product of my imagination—what had been bothering me for twelve hours surfaced: Sometimes white supremacy is simply having the audacity to tell a woman of colour that she cannot believe her own eyes or trust her own thoughts.

4.

In a series of text messages, my friend Justina and I pondered how we could take positive action. We didn't want to get depressed about the fact that our acquaintances could be so cavalier about hipster poverty tourism. What could we do besides give money to charity? After some thought, we settled on volunteering at a food bank.

5.

Over the weekend following these events, I watched a video of Canadian NDP leadership hopeful Jagmeet Singh at an event, prior to his win.

He's in a suit paired with a gloriously golden turban. A white woman is shaking her finger in his face, screaming about Sharia law.

The woman continues to colonize the space with her hate. He remains calm.

Singh responds, "We welcome you, we support you, and we love you.... we all believe in your rights."

What else could he have done? If he had elected to do anything in retaliation, the media would have called him a thug and destroyed his career. They would have found a picture of him sparring at a martial arts competition—lit in low light to make his skin appear darker—to run during the twenty-four hour news cycle. He had no choice but to shine with compassion, love, and courage. This is who he is, so he was able to overcome with grace. It saddens me that he—like all other people of colour—must always be graceful, must always go high when others go so very low, or risk losing everything.

After the incident, Singh released a statement: "I chose not to answer the questions asked because I didn't accept the premise. Many people have commented that I could have just said I'm not Muslim. In fact, many have clarified that I'm actually Sikh. While I'm proud of who I am, I purposely didn't go down that road because it suggests their hate would be OK if I was Muslim. We all know it's not."

6.
In The Gift of Fear, Gavin de Becker writes, "It is understandable that the per-

spectives of men and women on safety are so different—men and women live in different worlds...at core, men are afraid women will laugh at them, while at core, women are afraid men will kill them."

Along similar lines when it comes to safety white and non-white people live in different worlds. As people of colour we must be ever so careful about the fragile feelings of the racists who want us dead. At core we think they will kill us, so we must either stay silent or lead with love. We know they will murder us even though we are minding our own business and the law will be on their side. In news reports the pictures of us that flash across the screen look like mug-shots even when we are the victim, even when we are a cadaver laid out in the morgue. There is no winning this rigged game.

7.

The friend of [redacted] did not contact me to apologize for the emotionally charged statements he had directed at me. Instead, days later he commented on Facebook again because was unhappy that I had posted M. Paramita Lin's searing essay "Everybody Hates a Tourist", which compares hipster poverty role play with court entertainment: "French queen Marie Antoinette built a faux farm in Versailles called Hameau de la Reine where she and her buddies could pretend to be shepherdesses and milkmaids while still living a thousand times better than the actual peasants."

When I didn't respond to the man, he sent me a private message. He felt he was the injured party, that I was supporting the misrepresentation of his character. I understood why he was upset, but I wondered who or what had taught him that he could act the fool and expect that I yield to him. Why did he think I was responsible for soothing his hurt feelings? For what reason did he believe he was entitled to my time after his incivility?

Here we were, trapped in the same cycle of suffering: "Each time it begins in the same way, it doesn't begin the same way, each time it beings it's the same."

I saw my path: if I wanted to escape the same, there was nowhere for me to go except in the direction of love and courage. This was not a high-minded or commendable decision, nor was it an attempt to protect white feelings; I did it to save myself from succumbing to the hot rage that is always threatening to drown me. There was nothing to do but draw upon loving kindness to wish this man joy and peace like I was some kind of demented holiday greeting card.

I chose not to accept the premise so that I could walk away, free. Alive.

¹ Claudia Rankine, "Stop-and-Frisk." Here the poet is writing about how black men get stopped by law enforcement. I acknowledge that these life and death situations make an online encounter between two people seem pretty silly. I have the privilege of making a choice for my own mental health, while none of these men are afforded this basic right.

Doretta Lau   079

Jesús Maya

Jesús Maya's poetry explores two main themes: urban life in San Agustin, Ecatepec, Mexico where he grew up and the experience of migration including the crossing of borders, the separation of families, and vulnerabilities that ensue from those processes.

His poetry has been published in two anthologies: *Iguana: Writing Exile/Iguana: Escribir el Exilio* (Enana Blanca Press, 2008) *and Lumbre y Relumbre: Antologia Selecta de la Poesia Hispanocanadiense* published (Editorial Antares, 2013). His firsl sole authored book, *La Tolvanera* was first published as a Spanish-only edition by the Latin American Researchers of Ontario and presented at Inspire! Toronto International Book Fair in 2014. His writings have been musicalized, audio recorded, published in electronic media as well as newspapers and magazines. They also inspired a short film titled *Canciones*.

J
E
Ṣ
Ú
S

M
A
Y
A

Toronto (Spanish)

Ayer soñé que
pintábamos con
pintura acrílica
azul marino.

Soñé que pintábamos,
hacíamos los cortes,
rolábamos.

Y limpiamos con Windex
unas gotas que
habían caído al piso
de goma.

El aroma
me recordó a ti,
el letargo del trabajo...

Soñaba que ya no estamos en México
y no éramos
ninguno de los 72 asesinados y asesinadas en Tamaulipas.
.

Que nos tocábamos nuestras carnes.

Toronto

Last night I dreamed
that we were painting
with acrylics,
ocean blue.

I dreamed that we were painting
cutting the borders
rolling the walls.

With Windex we cleaned
a few drops
that had fallen
to the rubber floor.

The aroma
reminded me of you,
the exhaustion of my job...

I dreamed we were no longer in Mexico
and that we were not among
the 72 murdered men and women
in Tamaulipas.

That we pinched our own flesh, relieved

No éramos parte de los 72,
ni de los 400 que caen todos los años,
ni de los miles que son puntos en el mar.
Arizona es solo una noticia.

Soñé que tú y yo cabíamos aquí,
que no fuimos plantados en Toronto.
Toronto.
Tenemos sangre, lágrimas,
mucho miedo.
Y también sentimos dolor,
de ese que no se quita

nunca.

that we were not among those 72
or those 400 that fall every year
nor those thousands who are now just specks on the sea.
Arizona is one mere segment of the news.

I dreamed that you and I might actually fit in here,
that we weren't just dropped here in Toronto.

Blood, tears,
and many fears
run through us.
And we feel so much pain,
the kind that doesn't stop
ever.

Verdad

Mamá...
Ya no hay que temerle a la pandilla,
ya no tienes que preocuparte...
Cuando llega la noche estoy en casa,
esperando a que llegues de trabajar.

Mamá ¡Se ha roto el ciclo!
Mamá tu hijo no pasará...
¡Lo que han vivido todas tus generaciones!

Mamá no tendré que ser campesino.
Mamá no seré borracho.
¡Mamá no seré más naco indio!

Mamá podré ir a la universidad.
Mamá comeremos carne roja.
¡Mamá aquí nadie inhala pegamento!

Mamá aquí no tendrás miedo
de encontrarme en un charco de sangre.

Mamá, ¿verdad que no es cierto?
¿Que a nadie le importa si soy Latino?
¿Verdad mamá que aquí no existe la "migra"?

Right, Mamá?

Mamá...
Now you don't have to be afraid of gangs.
You don't have to worry.
When night falls, I'm at home
waiting for you to come back from work.

Mamá, the cycle has been broken!
Your son won't have to experience
the pain your past generations endured.

Mamá, I won't have to be a farmer.
Mamá, I won't be a stumbling drunk.
Mamá, I won't be another ghetto Indian!

Mamá, I'll be able to go to university
Mamá, we'll eat red meat.
Mamá, over here no one gets high on glue!

Mamá, here you won't have to worry
about finding me in a pool of blood.

Mamá, isn't it true
that no one will be bothered that I'm Latino?
They don't have the "migra" here, right?

¿Verdad mamá que a la policía no le importa mi raza?

¿Verdad mamá que en nuestra comunidad no hay delatores?

¿Verdad que tus compañeros de trabajo no te preguntan por tu situación migratoria?

¿Verdad que tu compañera de casa es de confianza?

¿Verdad que todo va a salir bien?

¿Verdad que aquí la gente se acerca con buenas intenciones?

¿Verdad que hay mucha gente buena?

Mamá,

¿Verdad que son puros rumores que inventa la gente?

¿Verdad que vemos cosas que no existen?

¿Verdad que cuando salgas al trabajo vas a regresar?

¿Verdad que no entra migración a las cafeterías?

¿Verdad que el primer ministro entiende lo que es empezar desde abajo?

¿Verdad mamá que pagan salarios justos?

¿Verdad que a las agencias de empleo les importa tu vida?

¿Verdad que saben que los inmigrantes llenamos las fábricas?

¿Verdad que saben quién construyó sus casas?

¿Que nosotros los inmigrantes somos formas de vida más complejas?

¡No somos embajadores de países sucios, corruptos, muertos de hambre, peligrosos!

¿Verdad que si te casas por amor se arregla todo?

¿Verdad que sabes de muchas buenas noticias?

Aren't the police colourblind?

No one's going to tell on us, right?

Isn't it true that your coworkers don't ask you about your status?

And your roommate is trustworthy?

And everything is going to work out just fine?

Isn't it true that here people only approach you in good faith?

Aren't most people here good?

Mamá,

We've just been hearing made-up rumours, right?

Aren't we just imagining things?

When you leave your job, you'll be able to go back, right?

Immigration officials don't come into coffee shops, right?

Doesn't the Prime Minister understand what it means to start from nothing?

Mamá, don't they pay fair wages here?

Don't employment agencies care about our safety?

Aren't people aware that we immigrants fill the factories?

Don't they know who built their houses?

Aren't we immigrants more complex forms of life?

We're not the ambassadors of dirty, corrupt, hungry, dangerous shithole countries!

If you marry for love, everything will fall into place, right?

You hear plenty of good news, right?

Because there's a lot of good news! Isn't there?

¡Porque hay muchas buenas noticias! ¿Verdad que sí?

¿Verdad que Dios ve todo lo que pasa?

...Si ponemos nuestra vida a su cuidado ¿nada pasará?

¿Verdad que es mentira que la corrupción aquí es legal?

¿Verdad que si no estás más conmigo no se va a acabar el mundo?

¿Verdad mamá que la delación no es promovida y recompensada?

¿Verdad que nuestra comunidad es unida y se ayuda?

¿Verdad mamá que nada es verdad?

¿Verdad mamá que todo es mentira?

¿Verdad que no vas a llorar?

¿Verdad que nos vamos a extrañar?

¿Verdad que todo es un sueño?

¿Verdad que todo es un mal sueño?

¿Verdad que solo estamos viviendo un mal sueño?

¿Verdad que tú y yo no somos unos pobres soñadores?

God sees everything that happens, right?

...And if we place our lives in his care, how can anything go wrong?

Aren't people lying when they say corruption is legal here?

Isn't it true that if you're no longer with me, the world won't come to an end?

It can't be real that turning people in is encouraged and rewarded.

Aren't our people united, helping one another?

So, Mamá, is nothing really true?

Is everything just a lie?

You're not going to cry, right?

We're going to miss each other?

This is all just a dream, right?

A bad dream?

We're just living in a bad dream, right?

Aren't we more than bad dreamers?

Mi Mundo Visto desde el Ground Floor

Esta mañana llegó la "migra"
a mi trabajo.
Uniforme gris, documentos,
con fotografía en mano.

Me preguntaron
si conocía a la persona del apartamento 608,
no recuerdo el nombre.

"OK. ¿Ve usted ese edificio
color café?
Pues ahí no es, vaya más adelante
y de vuelta a la derecha, al East",
pensé...

"Hasta encontrar la primera autopista
y diríjase hacia el sur,
hasta llegar a la primera intersección..."

"Estacione su auto en cualquier lugar
y camine, olvide.
Consígase un trabajo de verdad,
siniestro y repugnante personaje."

My world as seen from the ground floor

This morning the "migra" showed up
at my workplace.
Grey uniforms, documents,
a photograph in hand.

They asked me
if I knew the person from
apartment 608,
I don't recall his name.

"OK, do you see this building?
The brown one?
That's not it, go over there
turn right, toward the East"
I thought...

"Until you reach the first highway
and then head south
until you hit the first intersection..."

"Park your car anywhere
and walk, forget.
Get yourself a real job
you creepy, despicable character."

Pero únicamente le sonreí
mientras, mirándole a los ojos,
le respondí que no...
no conocía a quien buscaba.
En inglés, claro.

That's what I wanted to say
but instead I just smiled
while, staring into his eyes,
I said no—
I didn't know who he was looking for—
in English, of course.

Sheena Kamal

Sheena Kamal received the Kobo Emerging Writer Prize and the Strand Magazine Critics Award for her debut thriller *The Lost Ones*, which was a national bestseller. The sequel *It All Falls Down* was released 2018, and the third installment of the series will be published in 2020, along with a YA novel set in her hometown of Toronto.

Sticky Issues and The Absent Latina

I guess I've never felt comfortable in my own skin. Well, I shouldn't say never. I was doing okay up until the age of six, when my family immigrated to Canada and threw what I'd known of my identity into flux. Also, in the past few years, after two of the most meaningful friendships of my life utterly disintegrated, I have found a measure of solace in rediscovering who I am in the absence of two of my most steadfast pillars. This is just what life is and, hopefully, a person can grow into herself as it moves along.

But in those twenty-five odd years in the middle, I have looked for clues about my identity in same places that most lonely misfits do: the arts.

According to my family, I've been a storyteller since I could speak, but my approach to storytelling has changed over the years. Though I'm now a novelist, I'd initially wanted to create and participate in stories to be played out on screen. I owe this ambition largely to the Toronto International Film Festival, which I'd been introduced to during college.

TIFF quickly became one of the highlights of my year. I could only afford to see one film per festival year and would eagerly pore over film descriptions, making lists and shortlists. Every fall presented an opportunity to see movies that would never get wide distribution, but were still a window into places I thought I'd never go. The festival was where I first saw *The Wind That Shakes The Barley* and fell in love with the Irish landscape. Where I saw *The Sapphires* and went mad for Australia. Same with Tsotsi and South Africa. *Atanarjuat* and the Arctic.

You get the picture. Like all art, films can show you the human experience in new ways. A balance between truth and imagination. For a diminutive Caribbean transplant who, after years of living in Canada still had no clue how to adjust to life here, exploration of self through art was essential. I wanted to read every book ever written. I wanted to watch films about all sorts of people and places, beyond the usual Hollywood fare. I wanted to see something of the world to help me figure out who I am and where I could possibly fit.

One year, I took a job at the festival as an assistant in one of the interview suites. The glitz and glamour were secondary to me. I was thrilled because I thought I'd get discounted tickets. Maybe even see a few films. I was nurturing my budding writing aspirations back then, and I thought spending time at the festival would help feed my imagination. It always had before. There was a particular film I'd been interested in, which was set to be the festival darling. There is one every year, and it usually goes onto be nominated for the Academy Awards, as well as making the other festivals on the circuit. That year the darling was a stylized action flick with an A-list cast—and one of my favourite actors in the world was in it. I was so excited. I take unparalleled delight in action flicks. They can be so cheesy—but I love them.

The film was based on a book, which I immediately put on my to-read list. The screenings were sold out, so I wouldn't be able to see it at the festival (and there were no discounted tickets that came with the gig, as I'd previously thought) but I was able to tag along to the interview with this director I wanted so badly to meet. I thought it would be the highlight of my week. I'd learned that the festival itself looks exciting from the outside but it is, in actuality, an exercise in mind-numbing tedium. Both the talent and the people who run the interviews and events are stuck in windowless rooms for hours on end, talking for hours and saying absolutely nothing at all. For some reason, however, I'd expected the interview with this director, this visionary, to be different—and it was.

During the interviews the director was asked why he changed the ethnicity of the love interest. In the book, she'd been a Latina but he'd hired a blonde British actress to play the part. I perked up. I hadn't known this little casting tidbit. His response to the question was stunning. He said he couldn't find any Latina actresses that he'd felt protective of and he wanted to avoid any 'sticky race issues' when it came to the on-screen romance.

This shocked me. It shouldn't have, but it did. In truth, I had expected something from him and I wasn't disappointed. Well, I was, but in a completely different way.

A little context might be helpful here. The story he'd brought to the screen is set in Los Angeles, where there is a large Hispanic population. The author of the novel thought it was necessary to have a Latina character to represent that... and along comes this director who, with one fell swoop, erased the only non-white woman from the narrative because of his own personal biases—which he freely admitted to!

I suddenly understood something that I'd been missing for a while, why I'd unconsciously turned to arthouse and international cinema for clues to my own identity. Why I hardly ever found them in popular film and television—or in popular literature, for that matter. That day, I saw that the status quo doesn't have to be particularly nefarious. It is simply easier. It's easier to write and create in your own image than it is to delve into 'sticky race issues'—and those of gender, class and sexual orientation. You know, the stuff that makes people who they are.

The brilliant rapper and actor Riz Ahmed recently gave a speech to British Parliament where he talked about the importance of representation. He spoke of how meaningful it is to him as an actor of Pakistani origin to be thought of, to be considered. What if his outstanding performance in HBO's *The Night Of* was swapped out because of sticky race issues? If those issues hadn't been highlighted, how flat would the story have been?

When I finally got around to watching the film, I didn't enjoy it. I found that the presence of one of my favourite actors of all time couldn't bring back my excitement for this movie. The love interest was just that. She seemed to have no other function than to be a prop. It was not an inspiring part for any actress but, perhaps because I'd heard the director's take on casting the female lead, I often think of that absent Latina. What kind of film could it have been if she'd been considered? How would it have changed the story? Why did the director need to feel protective of her in the first place?

And, quite unhelpfully, in terms of my own identity and the way it is perceived in this world, am I as easily erased as she'd been? When I look in the mirror, I am generally okay with who I see staring back at me. I mean, it would be great to be taller and more beautiful, but I've come to terms with the fact that I'm not taller and more beautiful. So, I'm okay with my reflection. However, after that festival year, I couldn't help but think that in this director's world, like the Latina, I might not exist.

That interview moment raised all sorts of uncomfortable questions and troubled me greatly at the time, but I didn't realize how much of an impact it had until several years later when I began writing *The Lost Ones*, my debut suspense novel. I didn't shake my fists at the heavens and vow that I would be inclusive when it comes to my own writing. I actually tried to forget about that experience, but it had marked me. The book showed me just how much I think about representation. When I write, I think about the place I've chosen as a setting. Who are the people that I find there? How can I try to do them justice and make this real? It's not always pleasant to put myself in a place of uncertainty as to whether I've approached a character's identity in a compassionate way, but I'd rather flame out spectacularly in the attempt than not try.

In *The Lost Ones*, I didn't shy away from difficult subjects simply because I don't always like to talk about them. I don't expect any sort of prize for this, by the way. To each her own. As it was with those films that I'd gone to the festival to see, that I studied listings to find, I just wanted to give a real sense of the place the story is set. I want to see both truth and imagination play out in my world. I would have been unhappy with myself if I'd gone in any other direction, you see, because I felt I owed some consideration to someone who had been erased once. The absent Latina isn't absent to me. In a weird way, after all these years, it turns out she's been guiding my pen.

Mary Pinkoski

Mary Pinkoski, 5th Poet Laureate of the City of Edmonton (2013-2015), is an internationally recognized poet. She has performed on stages across North America and Europe and her work has appeared in anthologies. Mary was the 2019 Edmonton Public Library Regional Writer in Residence, the 2011 Canadian National Spoken Word Champion, and the 2008 CBC National Poetry Face-off winner. In 2015, Mary was recognized as an Edmonton Top 40 Under 40 and also awarded a University of Alberta Alumni Horizon Award for her poetry work in the Edmonton community, in particular for her creation of the City of Edmonton's Youth Poet Laureate role.

Let the Ghosts Out: A suite of poems

One.

You are a long, glaring splinter I pull from myself
Your entry and exit wounds are happiness
So I am not sure from where it is that you originate

How tightly must I have had to hold on to this
For it to embed itself into me

You are the long, glaring red rescue rope I pull from myself
With the muscle memory of seamstress
Worrying together her first animal

Anais Nin said anxiety is love's greatest killer.

I have read that the perfectly pruned olive tree
Is one with enough spaces in between its branches
For a sparrow to fly through without hitting its wings

Held sacred as symbols of peace by the ancient Greeks
There are people in this world who stand like olive trees
People whose hearts do not double-dutch

Whose breath does not race

People who move gracefully through the uncertainties of life

Making awkward shrubs of the rest of us

Most of us are not this kind of perfectly pruned tree

We come into this world bent over from limbs laden with life

Less like stoic control and more like a frantic frenzy

We are tripped up by the easy moments of this world

And we break from hearts that long for stillness

And breaths that seek metronomes

I have known this rapid pace

But right now, I am just standing here waiting for a prayer

Written beyond a windbreak of perfectly pruned olive trees

A place where the fracturing is not so horrible

Where the morning splits like in a Cat Steven's song

Where the last thunder in a storm cracks

Where branches laden with fruit tumble into an easy faint

Where the wave breaks like a fever against the harbour

It is sweet sacrifice coming to understand

Your futility to the fervor of this life

It is the revelation of a slow religion when we realize

We will never be olive trees worth worshiping

Our bodies forever holding awkward gracelessness like an intention,

And still, we let the sparrows of life fly into us
Knowing there is not exit route

There are no temples in this shrubbery
Our bodies are not worth the shrines
We are nothing more than dilapidated shelters
Seeking small mercies
Like a sparrow choosing to nest in our branches

Anais Nin said anxiety makes others feel as you might
When a drowning man holds on to you

I do not know if
I am more in love with the moon or with the tide
With the return or with the escape

In the bathtub
My hair is a tangled empty net
I wish my heart were less moon
I wish my love was less tidal

Anais Nin said you will want to save the drowning man
But you know he will strangle you with his panic

There will be a flood soon
The ocean will come to me
And I will swim

For I have never learned not to swim
When the flood arrives

Which is to say,
When this body of water opens
Itself up to me

Rushing through the cracks in my body
Pouring down inside of my being
I do not know how not to try and swim out of it

Which is to say,
I am trying to swim out of my body
Which is to say,
I have never learned not to try and swim out of my body

Which is to say again,
I am trying to swim out of myself

Which is to say,
I am drowning

Which is to say,
I am so spilling with story

I long to become the thin slip of a paper boat
A set of paper instructions on how to escape

Two.

Instructions

1. The poet Tara Hardy was right in *Adam's rib there is a kitchen*. Remember: in the kitchen there is a stove and on the stove is a gas burner. Love the woman whose hand controls the burner, the suicidal desires of gas. Do not let Adam's rib become a bell jar.

2. In the kitchen there is an apple. In the apple there is a choice. In choice there is the body of a woman eating sweet fruit. In the kitchen there is a woman who is finally full; licking her lips.

3. Outside the kitchen window there is grass. In the grass there is a serpent.

4. In the serpent's eye is the woman. We could call her eve or we could call her naked.

5. Once, in Adam's rib there was a kitchen, and in the kitchen there was a genesis and in genesis there is birth and in birth there is always a Woman.

Three.

In Montreal's Notre Dame
There is a candle that refuses to stop burning

Behind Victoria's Royal Roads Military College
There is a tree that has not stopped growing

When the women in my family speak of where they are from
They do not say here
They say there

Cooking in her kitchen in the middle of an Edmonton winter
My nana sings Gilles Vigneault
"mon pays ce n'est pas un pays/c'est l'hiver"
My mom sings the Pauls—McCartney and Simon—
These women are a kettle's whistle of solo albums

When they say home,
They do not say here
They say Montreal or Victoria
They say longing and missing

Born under wheat field air,
I am the first generation of women in my family
To not know what it is like to have another place in my body

Still they feed me tortiere and strawberry shortcake
Tiny cups of tea and giant paintings of Emily Carr

Until they are empty

And I am so full up of them
I am spilling

Four.

Take this holy. This bar stool blessing. This final swig of beer. Take this cross.
This hill. This garden. This darkness. Take this light. Take this doubting Thomas.
Take this closing door. Take this open tomb. Take this stone. Take this fist. Take
this dove. Take this wave. This boat. This night without a lighthouse. Take this
metal upon metal. Take this accident. This spilled milk. Take this mistake. Take
this one good thing that I did. Take this breath. This heart beat. Take this one
music note I never invented. Take this sound. Take this silence. Take this cup that
refuses to run over. Take this seeping. Take this spilling.

Five.

Anne Waldman asks how much backward from your own death do you write?

And just now, I wanted to write you of the way
the wolves will lick your neck before they bite

The way the waves will lull you back and forth
Before their force pulls you under

The drowning do not know their own strength
And I am no sturdy rope tied for the pull of a rescue
No knot fraying under urgent stress

I wanted to write you of the land before the flood
I wanted to write you of the ocean before the water
I wanted to write you of the body before the stories

Six.

I imagine that at some point in the storm,
God must tire of the thunder and the chaos
His hands must take some joy in untwisting the struggle
And turning the world changed,
But unchanged,
Back into itself

I imagine the story of my body
Is just as much there in my presence
As it is in my absence

Some day, I will come across this poem
And mistake its drowning to be swimming

After all water is just water
No matter how it twists and untwists

So why then splatter these walls with storm and thunderclap

Why not blue the walls with a shade of respite

Why not play God
Or storm

For just moment:
Untwist the water
Turn the knob
Blow the door open

Let the ghosts out

S
A
R
A

T
I
L
L
E
Y

Sara Tilley

Sara Tilley's work bridges writing, theatre, and Pochinko clown through mask. She's published two award-winning novels: *Skin Room* (Pedlar Press, 2008), and *DUKE*, (Pedlar Press, 2015), and written, co-written or co-created twelve plays. She lives in St. John's, Newfoundland and Labrador, Canada. Find her at saratilley.ca.

Crystal

It was nearly a year since they ended it, and all Carrie could think about was Phantom Baby. Phantom Baby doesn't cry, it goes 'boo'. Phantom Baby doesn't need to be changed, it changes you.

The baby is made of mist, but the mist is like coral, porous and hollow, and its nooks and crannies have sponged up real baby's blood, so that this blood-baby thingy is red but gauzy, wet but nothing, and it floats. It follows Carrie, sometimes from very far away, sometimes hiding behind buildings so that she can't see it anymore, though she can still feel the tug—a twinge in the weak side of her left wrist, not dissimilar to the ache, in poor weather, of a badly-set broken bone.

Phantom Baby came in a dream at first, one or two days after they were done. Carrie wasn't sleeping in the house. She'd given him a week to get his things out. She was at her friend's place, her old friend from childhood, her only real pre-Martin friend, Ginny, who was back in town for just that one summer out of the whole decade beforehand, so it seemed like The Universe had Carrie cradled to Its Universal Teats even as her sternum cracked with so much crying. Literal heartbreak! It actually made cracking sounds, like the river ice in springtime in Dawson City, where they had lived together once, Martin and Carrie, True Love Forever, the kind everyone else is jealous and suspicious of.

Carrie left Newfoundland two months ago. She knows that he left, too. London. He's really doing it, now that he doesn't have her weighing him down. In the old days, he'd joke about the tattoo he was planning to get—an anchor, with Carrie's name on it.

Martin, in London. She tries not to care. She only knows because of Facebook. Not because they're Friends—he removed her—but because they have Friends in common, and when he Comments on a Friend's Post it will sometimes show up in her Feed, like a hand reaching out of the computer screen and dumping a cold glass of water on her. Today, someone Shared this photo of him with his girlfriend. She's short, and young, with no detectable thickening of her anatomy. Martin is smoking, looking straight at the camera with a neutral expression, while GF turns to look up at him, her mouth half-opened as if she's about to say something, or maybe kiss him, or like she's his baby bird and he'll regurgitate a worm for her. She sees only Martin, and he only sees us. The two of them are wearing black on a British bridge, overlooking the British water.

In that dream Carrie had, in Ginny's parents' spare bed, one of those first dark nights a year ago when she dove gratefully into sleep like Ophelia—get at me, Death!—she dreamt that she and Martin were on a bus, though he looked not like himself but like a younger man with lighter hair, a teenager. They were on the bus nearing the house where she used to live as a girl. They had bags of shopping at their feet—Value Village—and her wrist was very itchy. Carrie scratched. No matter how diligent, she couldn't get rid of the itch in her wrist, her left wrist, on the soft part, underneath. A rash began to bloom, red as blood in a sponge, dark and serious. On skin so pale as hers you could see it extra clearly: the silhouette of a fetus in classic fetal position rising up on her wrist, on the tender underside part, red and itchy, bubbled like a sponge of blood, growing more and more pronounced as the seconds passed, about two inches long between the furthest points of its half-formed anatomy.

'Holy shit', she said in the dream. She grabbed Martin's arm. 'We're pregnant. Isn't it beautiful?' The red fetus-rash-thing winked a pre-eye, eye-nub, head-of-a-matchstick at her and opened its economic slash of a pre-mouth right below its two tiny pinholes of pre-nostrils. It smiled, and said its name was Crystal.

Martin's stand-in was uncomfortable. He wouldn't look Crystal in the 'eye'. He put his head- phones on—it was Pulp—and even though they were expensive, earmuff ones, the music now underscored everything. He got off the bus, and Carrie followed him. The breeze picked up. Crystal began to blow away. She was light as a feather, so small, a mere two inches from top to tail. Carrie ran after her and called for Martin to run too—'grab the baby, the baby's going to float away, Martin'—but he had gone inside and she could see him through the window at the table. Her mother, aged thirty or so in the dream, was feeding him lasagna. There was a tugging on Carrie's wrist. A vein, snaking up! One had come loose, snagged in her scratching. The vein tugged right out of her wrist and up into the sky, a kite-string from Carrie to her floating daughter.

Crystal loved the wind. She sucked it greedily into her little half-lungs. She was a sponge for it, expanding quickly like one of those vitamin-looking capsules you put in a pail of water, as a child, to grow a foamy dinosaur. Crystal swelled in the wind till she took up the whole sky and the sun shone through her like stained glass. She was so beautiful. Her cells grew bigger and bigger until they were a cathedral ceiling of crimson wonders, a bisected, glowing pomegranate of perfection, and it was easier to see the space between each cell, and between each thing within each cell, all that space that's in all of us but which is easier to see if you are a huge balloon-Phantom Baby-fetus-thing that never really existed, and that appears in a dream.

The Baby is often there in the daytime, too. When in public, Carrie pretends not to notice. No one else notices. Phantom Baby is exceptionally bright for a thing of her age. She'd never appear when someone else might see, not unless Carrie ran into Martin, which hadn't happened, not even randomly, all year. A miracle, really, considering St. John's. Now that she's in Calgary and he's in the UK, Carrie guesses she'll never see Martin again, though you never know. The art world, in his words, is 'pretty fucking small'.

All year, Carrie's lived with sadness. It's understandable, though her friends are getting restless. They encourage her to try online dating, swing dancing, gym membership. She doesn't know how to cut the cord without letting her blood out. And why cut it? Her sadness has a concrete form, better than the amorphous cloud she's seen swallow some in similar situations. Phantom Baby is better than a nameless, shapeless grief, unacknowledged until it ferments into cancer. Phantom Baby is an impossibility, yes, but even so she laughs, her laugh is on the wind, it's in the songs of birds, a distraction. She helps Carrie fall into the cotton batting feeling of forgetting.

There are some days that she doesn't think of him at all, and others when she conjures him up on purpose, dwelling on the way things might have been, if only, if only, like a tongue rooting at the raw hole of a recent wisdom tooth extraction. Her life was once so caught up with his. They used to be a thing together, a single unit, even in her dreams. It's hard, now, to remember the happy, early years. All tinged with the stuff at the end. Maybe that's the kind of thing where you have to wait to be old.

Phantom Baby is usually about a foot long. Real-baby-size. But when she laughs her impossible laugh and gulps the wind and begins to swell and fill the whole sky with her cells again, like in the dream, Carrie knows that a migraine is coming. The size of her baby is a weather vane. As the months kept on and the lawyers were called, the papers were drawn, and everything became quite final, Carrie found it too sad to think of Crystal with a name anymore, like she was a real baby who'd really existed, so Carrie just thought of her as Phantom Baby now, at least most of the time. When she's tired, or in a lot of pain, she occasionally slips, and thinks 'Crystal' to herself. She can feel Phantom Baby, can feel the tug, even while she's in the studio, or in the shower, at the grocery store, while cooking or out walking the unfamiliar city blocks, and of course while sitting and crying alone. She could feel Phantom Baby all the while, this whole year, tug-tug-tugging on the vein, her kite-string. No matter how far Carrie follows, Phantom Baby still keeps tugging. All the way across the country. How far are we to go?

It was a little over a year ago that he'd brought up getting pregnant, after a long while of not talking about it. They'd had sex that afternoon and were lying on the bed and hugging. A freeze-dried moment. Martin was tracing up and down her arm with his fingers and giving her little kisses on the hairline. He said they should start planning out when they'd have their kid, for real, because soon it would be too late for Carrie to do it, and if they were going to Calgary this coming year it should be conceived either in the next two months to make it old enough to travel, or they should wait to conceive until halfway through her residency so that she wouldn't be so pregnant they'd be worried about flying home. Even though Martin hated Newfoundland and everything about it, he wanted his child to be born there. He'd been thinking about it a lot, it seemed, and she was happy that he wanted it, really wanted it, and wanted her still, even though sometimes things got weird and hard and she didn't know what was wrong and he hit his head on the walls and said she was making him want to kill himself. An ultimatum: 'If you want to make it so we never have sex, that's fine. Let's just be honest about it. I'm done. I still love you, I'm still in love with you, but if you want to have sex with me again you're going to have to do the work to make it happen.'

A kiss was not an acceptable beginning move. He'd screw his mouth into a tidy fortress of teeth. Sometimes when drunk he'd mimic her, grabbing her by the neck, slamming his mouth into hers, ramming the tongue in. 'You think that's sexy?' Or, when she didn't try so hard: 'You know how many numbers I get every shift? You're killing me. I have to fuck, you know, or I'm going to explode. No, you don't know, do you? That's the problem.'

She nearly always came. She never faked. She loved having sex with him and she wanted to have it more, not less. She said this sometimes, or wrote him letters, longhand, to that effect. 'Prove it, then.' When she tried to dress in slutty things, she was too nervous about it and he'd say she was just doing it for his sake and not because she was a genuinely sexual person. Then he'd shut himself in his office with a case of beer and his video games and smoke in there all night, even though he'd promised he wouldn't smoke in the house. When the costumes did work, he'd often rip the thing to shreds on the first go so that she couldn't wear it again—cheap mail-order crap—and later he'd be put off that she didn't wear the hot outfit and wanted to have sex with him, naked, or starting off in regular clothes. There was a specific thing he wanted, but he wouldn't say what. 'If you have to talk about it, it's not erotic.' He thought it would be a healthy step if more people were involved. She did claim she was bi. His theory was asexual. Was she really a dyke? It was okay if she was, they'd have a three-some. Or he could just watch. Orgy? Go poly? Why does that make her cry? 'I've never met anyone as fucked up as you about fucking, Carrie, you know that?'

She wanted to have sex, but it wasn't dirty enough. She wanted to have sex, but just with Martin. She was happy to have sex just with him, alone. He'd say 'I don't know what's wrong with you,' and she wouldn't know what to say back. This was when he was drinking. He only said these things late at night after drinking and then he couldn't stop, monologues he'd later have no memory of. He'd come home at six am and wake her up to say all kinds of things about how miserable he was. He'd say she was just like her mother, and he didn't mean the migraines, he meant she was the spit of her, repressed and frigid and stuck. Martin would tell her that no one else would've stayed with her this long, as fundamentally broken as she was, and Carrie would thank him for being so patient, so very patient with all her shortcomings and flaws. He'd say, 'How'd I get the shit luck to fall in love with you anyway? How'd I get the shit luck?' and she'd apologize. She meant it. Sometimes he'd threaten to hit her if she wouldn't hit him first.

'Just punch me in the face, just fucking punch me or I swear to God I'll kick the shit out of you'. She wouldn't, and he never did, either. When it got to that point, she'd retreat to the bathroom to sob with the door closed, letting Martin spew his thoughts, snort his drugs and pound his head into the wall until he felt like passing out.

Hit him? She guessed. Bought a riding crop for Christmas, wrapped it with a note that said to report to his French Teacher, he'd failed his examen de vocabulaire. She thought this was a way she could meet him where he needed to be met. The character would help. She'd get some use from her theatre degree, for once. Martin didn't even take the crop out of the box. 'I'm not into that shit.' She never saw it again. Shame freezing her up. He stayed out more and more and she got more and more sad. They touched each other less, and even their lives touched less, overlapping a little in the afternoon when she was finishing up in the studio for the day and he was starting to wake up. That was no time to try. Martin was tired. Hung over? It was his hour for email and coffee, a game of hockey on the Xbox. Then he had to iron his clothes for the upscale waiting job he hated, downtown. It was never the right time to say 'Let's fuck'.

And then? A pull at the wrist. Phantom Baby leads Carrie back to that particular day last year. A frozen day, trapped in amber, a perfect golden day when she thought she was wrong about everything because of the good sex they'd had, just regular sex that arose out of a little kiss, as it used to very easily, and then the hugging in the bed and the baby that Martin began to talk about again, in practical terms, like they were saving up for South America. If he hadn't made getting pregnant real again, it would've hurt less, she thinks, when some days later she found the letter—well, Facebook Letter—open on his laptop by the couch, where he'd fallen asleep with his hand down his pants. A letter to some person about her vulva and its virtues, its tastiness and addictiveness. When can he eat it again? There were a few moments of stillness, then, another little amber moment where nothing happened. He was passed out and pale with drinking, his shirt off and his mouth open, his hand on his cock. The Profile Pic showed a green wig, fake lashes, black corset. A classic Selfie, the duck-face shot from above to cartoonishly enlarge the eyes while still including crucial cleavage—the type of shot that'd usually get Martin ranting, pacing up and down the living room kicking a book across the floor, skewering whatever friend of his was idiot enough to take that kind of picture of themselves and post it on the internet.

Carrie stood with her hand over her mouth for a while, and then she watched that hand shake him awake. She watched from way up high somewhere while he quickly flipped things. What was he supposed to do, she was fucking killing him. He was drunk and maybe coked up. It was eight in the morning. He said that even though she made him want to fucking slit his wrists he'd have stayed with her until the end. 'I'd be miserable for the rest of my life for you.' There were a lot more things he said, but those are the things that float to the surface now, when she thinks about it.

Carrie knows that out of all the many things he said, some were true, and some were meant to hurt her. She never knew which was which, and in the end it didn't matter. He said it all. She agreed with him. Some feminist! There were these ruts in her brain, old tracks laid down since girlhood. Carrie apologized for her incurable frigidity, the catalyst for Martin's conquest. She felt bad for him, for his belief in his own worthlessness, his own neural ruts, worn smooth as bobsled runs, that made him act this way. She knew she had to leave him, and she only had the strength to do it because of Ginny, who'd come back just this one summer to housesit for her newly-retired, newly-globetrotting parents. Ginny was an angel sent to hold Carrie while everything was swept away, as in a floodplain situation. Half her adult life was gone in that one moment, eight years and a bit, the million I love you's, the home they made, the work they made together; Carrie had to tie it all up and put it outside and cut it off and smush it because she could see now that she didn't really know Martin, and that if she did come to know him, the real him, then maybe she wouldn't actually love him. She didn't know this man, Martin, anymore.

They say it takes seven years for a lover to fully make their way out of a person's system. Some Facebook linky-thingy told her that. Carrie can't wait that long. She mostly feels nothing, but sometimes she has these unbearable waves of sadness when she thinks about him, or sees some Post about his book or his art show or his girlfriend's ultrasound. Carrie can well up if she sees someone put their hand on the back of their lover's neck, or if Nick Cave comes on shuffle, or if her cabbie smells of Ivory soap, tobacco, and artificial cinnamon. Those small candy hearts. It doesn't take much. A wave of terrible loss smacks into her and knocks her breath out. Then come the tears, in snotty torrents which are hard to stop. Self-worth bottomed out. Cannot look in mirror, trouble going to supermarket. Meals eaten over sink, for easier cleanup.

She finds herself scratching sometimes, her under-wrist getting red and puffy with the suffering, but it feels good to feel something relatively simple. A pain that is just scratches. Concentrate! Feel the teensy heartbeat. Scratch out the shape of her, focus in. Scratch in time to the wee breath. It is the breath of the last thing in this world made by the both of them—one last fucked-up, fictitious collaboration. She wants Crystal to follow her forever, fluttering in the treetops, but she also wants to cut that vein-string. A deft snip with psychic vibrations or legitimate scissors, whatever works.

Carrie wants to rest. She wants out of the city. Too loud. She wants some pure dark place, some cave, a spongy forest floor, somewhere without stars, or okay, maybe a few stars, but nothing else. No human structures on the dark land-scape, no people. No memories of people, no unborn small people, and no fully grown adults. Not even the thought that there could be people, somewhere. No sound. No sense of time. There's no one else, and there never has been, and there never will be. There's not even a you, not really, just a pure animal state, but one without a startle response, because there's nothing to be afraid of. No predators, no illness, no aging, no hunger, no worry. No self-awareness. No physical body. Release? Relief. A tiny perfect world of dark and stillness, like the period at the end of a lengthy sentence.

Jamaal Jackson Rogers

Jamaal Jackson Rogers is an award winning Poet Laureate, arts educator, creative entrepreneur, and performance artist. He has brought his work to audiences locally and internationally and his defining moments are when he makes intimate connections with his participants during his workshop exchanges and performance sets. His topics range from emotional maturity to social justice, from parenting to the human condition, while his works have been highlighted in festivals, documentaries and educational institutions. He resides in Ottawa, Canada, with his wife and family, using the capital and his performance studio, THE ORIGIN ARTS & COMMUNITY CENTRE as his launch pad to teach, mentor and advocate for the arts.

Medicine

She said, "Our diversity is our medicine."
She said, "Our diversity is our medicine."
Gathering all the beauty in the world in one unifying sentence
And how could I challenge her? When I have sampled a taste of
utopian togetherness; trading in a lens of ignorance for a culture of multiple expressions,
narratives and languages

When I was younger, I never spoke about how intense I studied the human condition
My earliest memories begin with my father's Guyanese shoulders
embracing my mother in moonlight shuffle
As if they had memorized a famous routine from a champion figure skating couple
When he would halt his waltz to kneel to the ground and tuck us in under blankets
that warmed our bodies from the bone cold floor
Hoping to make sense of complex emotions shown by world travelers and
globetrotters that would eventually settle on Canadian soil
Watching moments of contemplation flash like brainstorms only to transform
into revolutionary actions
Actions that would ultimately alter my understanding of what it
feels to know when one is home

Those were days when we first arrived to Ottawa
Shelters becoming natural habitats until this glowing city of growing
capital helped us back on our feet
In these days of decades past I would meet faces attached to stories that

carried history from all across earth's marvelous landscapes

It was on Elmira Drive and Iris street where I crossed cultures from everywhere

I found lodging in the communities that shared the same longing as me

Spoken in a language of triumph and resiliency

Witnessed in the silent pride of a Cambodian man's smile

Who hides the pain of all that he and his wife left behind to find new hope

in a country that promises a better life

He shows no teeth but his grin is chin high and his eyes beam with glory,

as if the future told him that eventually, it would all be worth the journey

A language that reflects the ancient family lineage recited from a Somali

mothers call for her children playing chase in the twilight of August's eve

As if tribe and siblings had the same meaning, she sings out names from

the corner of her mouth like I've never heard before,

Samatar, Abdi Fatah, Muhammad, Nasra

And all at once I can taste the camel milk flow from the horn of Africa

Sweeping peninsulas to exotic islands in the Caribbean

Where Haitian diasporic doorsteps play zouk and kompa

And elders hands fry fish and chicken drumsticks

Sizzling stoves blowing smoke through windows that would

invite the auditory senses into a euphoria of nostalgia and hospitality

When the Creole escapes from their throats

You can hear the resistance still chanting freedom songs from the motherland

mixed with the chance to start a new renaissance on the frontiers of a liberated land

It didn't take much for us to celebrate the everyday
And when special occasions came
Ceremonies to honour joyous commemorations
We danced the Lebanese Dabke as if it was taught to us through breath and lung
rituals that match the rhythm of the sacred loud and tabla
Or at least watched in awe as men with frames the size of goal posts
dipped low and leaped beyond whatever struggles their fellow countrymen
faced back home

All that I was searching for
From subtle sunrise, midday sunshine and moving well beyond the shimmering sunset
Could be captured in these intense interactions of harmonious rapture
A place where my heart could be embedded in the art of solidarity
And my understanding of our collective Canadian identity unraveled
in that single moment of affinity
When she said to me, "Our diversity is our medicine."

I will never know what memories she carried beneath her skin that would lead her
to share such welcoming empathy
An indigenous woman who spoke truth beyond her own history of genocide that
has robbed her of her rightful claim to reconcile home

Maybe it was her native traditions that reminded her that we are one once we
defeat the walls of ignorance and isolation
But in one unifying sentence
With wisdom beyond my experience

She showed me

That if we ever want to know how deep our beauty and empathy resides,

we shall see it in the hope, the healing, the stories, the joy,

that lies in a newcomers eyes.

Belonging

A compound word of sorts

The source of which is

Loaded with purpose

Our relationship a vehicle endorsed by the need to support emotional attachment

Its course

Is to "be" as in "to exist "

To "long" as in "to yearn"

A longing for existence

To be seen and heard as part of a collective

Yet accepted as individuals within our diverse social circles

Rich textures involving

Revolving

Evolving in a cycle of sharing

Trading

Creating

Speaking with conviction

Practicing inclusion

A
Y
E
L
E
T

T
S
A
B
A
R
I

Ayelet Tsabari

Ayelet Tsabari was born in Israel to a large family of Yemeni descent. Her first book, *The Best Place on Earth*, won the Sami Rohr Prize for Jewish Literature, and was a New York Times Book Review Editors' Choice. Her memoir, *The Art of Leaving* (HarperCollins) was published in February 2019.

Green

We are green. Everyone starts green. Even the mean sergeant whose well-worn, faded uniform looks as though it was tailor-made for her. Even she was green once. Our own khaki is stiff and bunches in undesired places; it does nasty things to our bums and it flattens our chest. Not that it matters. We're in an all-girls base in the middle of nowhere. There's no one to impress here but the cooks in the kitchen and they are not the kind of guys you want to impress. They are the kind of guys who were too lazy to fight, the ones who scored too low on their classification tests. At this point in our service we still think we can do better. We dream about dating officers and paratroopers and fighters and pilots, like in that saying, "The best men for pilotage, the best women for the pilots!"

We are eighteen and have just graduated from high school except for those of us who haven't. We've come from big cities and small developing towns and kibbutzim and villages. Our parents immigrated to this country from Morocco and Poland and Iraq and Russia and Ethiopia. They came chasing a dream we took for granted, oblivious to the price they paid, to what they left behind. We are the ingredients in this famous melting pot that is the Israeli mandatory army service.

The food in the kitchen makes us periodically sick. And then at least we don't have to do kitchen duty, which is the worst, worse even than cleaning toilets. The kitchen is a ravenous monster: the dishes never stop coming, and they become grosser in masses, the food all mashed together, food that wasn't appealing to begin with: meat from cans, chewy white bread, overcooked vegetables. At night, lying on metal beds in our darkened tents, we talk about food, conjure the scents of our mothers' cooking, and when we have an hour off we go to the cantina and stuff ourselves with chocolate and chips and commiserate about how fat we're going to get in the army, like our neighbour who gained twenty kilos sitting at a desk all day as a secretary in Jerusalem, or our cousin who got so fat she needed a new set of uniforms. Except those of us who are planning to continue training and become fighters or officers. We call those girls Poisoned. It's army slang for those who have the love of the military running through their veins.

We pick up the army slang quickly, had heard it from our older siblings and the boys we crushed on in high school, watching them return on weekends smelling like metal and sweat, looking even sexier in their heroic fatigue. We touched ourselves at night thinking about these boys in their uniform, the way the pants hung off their bums, barely held by their khaki belts, looking so much better than we ever would, because whoever designed these uniforms didn't think about the curving bodies of teenage girls who are going to sit on their fat asses in dreary offices all day long, wasting their best years serving coffee to middle-aged grabby hands officers in the guise of serving our country.

After one week, it already feels like there's nothing else in the world but this, like this is all we'll ever have. We get used to the dust in our nostrils and the sand in our cracks, to waking up early and running and doing drills. We don't remember high school. We don't remember dressing up and going out and flirting and drinking and boys. We don't remember sex. Except for the two girls in tent six who are having it. We can hear their stifled moans under the scratchy blankets and some of us blush and others laugh and say, "Wouldn't that be nice?" and we look at each other and then quickly away.

Some nights, for no good reason, our sergeant wakes us up at one or two a.m., shaking our tents, screaming at us to get dressed and make our beds in five minutes, or disassemble our Uzis and reassemble them again. "Sisyphic," says the curly-haired one who reads books by a flashlight every night, the beam on the outside of her blanket like a drunken one-eyed car. "Fucking bullshit is what it is," says the skinny one who plucks her eyebrows too thin. Some of us begin to sleep with our uniforms on, Uzis under pillows, disturbing our dreams.

One of us cries into her pillow every night, and sometimes in the middle of the day. One of us throws up after every meal and we all pretend we can't hear her retching into the toilet. One of us prays every morning and we know she didn't have to be here because religious girls are exempt, and we think it's cool or crazy that she chose to. One of us, the skinny one with the eyebrows, talks back to the sergeant one day and is sent to disciplinary court and it's only week one. One of us doesn't speak any Hebrew because she came from Russia just a few weeks ago and one day in first-aid class she bleeds on her chair because she got her period—the smeared red stain on the white seat like a trampled poppy—and didn't know how to tell the sergeant or if she could even speak.

One day while we clean our guns, the girl who cries puts the barrel in her mouth and pretends to pull the trigger. We all scream and beg her to stop and she laughs and says, "Relax! It's a joke." "I can't believe they gave you a gun," says the one who reads. "I can't believe they gave any of us guns." She tells us she won't serve in Gaza or in the West Bank, that she's willing to go to jail for that, and a couple of the girls switch beds because they don't want to sleep next to a filthy traitor. That night we feel the cold metal under our heads, the danger of it lurking for just a moment before sleep takes over like a black beast.

We miss our mothers. We miss our parents' home and the kitchens we know. We miss our little siblings who drive us crazy. We miss our showers and our toiletries. We miss our boyfriends, and sex, and attention. Some of us start to not care so much when the cooks flirt with us and even when the gross one makes sexist remarks we giggle like idiots even though we feel dirty and ashamed.

We each get a printout sheet with a list of positions we could do according to how we scored in the classification tests, and those of us with shorter lists fold them into our pockets and don't talk about it. The one who put the barrel in her mouth crumples the sheet and tosses it behind her back like she couldn't care less, and that night she ends up having sex with one of the cooks, standing against the creaking shelf in the storage room, and one of us sees them and tells everybody.

One of us wants to be an officer; one of us wants to be a sergeant; one of us wants to be a teacher; one of us wants to be secretary and be a "small head" and come home every day. One of us wants to be posted as far away from home—"that shithole"—as possible. The one who had sex with the cook talks about seeing an army shrink and pretending to be crazy so they would let her go. She says she's not cut out for this and we say, "None of us are, honey. None of us are."

On our last week, we stay up late talking. We lie on the grass and watch the stars, because many of us come from big cities where all you ever see is a faded version of this sky. Some of us start smoking right about then because we're soldiers now and all grown up and we want to belong. We say we'll stay in touch and write and visit. We say we'll never forget each other. We suddenly don't want basic training to end.

But basic training will end and we will forget. We will serve as secretaries and teachers and officers and sergeants. We will get new ranks sewn on our arms, and our uniform will fade, become less green, mould onto our widening hips. We will make new friends. Some of us will fall in love with officers and pilots and cooks and drivers. A few of us will get sexually harassed by our officers and one of us will complain and wish she hadn't. We will feel confined and used and increasingly bitter, and hate the army for stealing our youth, for reducing us to numbers and ranks. Except those of us who will love it—the order, the purpose, the ease of following procedures—and go on to make it a career.

Some of us won't make it to the end, like the anorexic who'll be released early because she lost too much weight, or the eyebrows girl who will spend most of her army service in jail, or the one who put the barrel in her mouth, who will eventually convince the army to dismiss her, but then will kill herself anyway—not with a gun, with pills—and none of us will even know because we didn't keep in touch. And the one who always prayed, who will die in a terrorist attack on a bus in Jerusalem and we will see her smiling face on the front page of the newspaper and find out that she went on to become an officer, played piano, was engaged to be married. When we open our albums to look for her face in pictures, names will elude us.

But on the night before it ends, before any of this happens, we hold onto each other, those girls whose army IDs are consecutive to ours and always will be, bonded by these strange circumstances. We rest our heads on each other's shoulders, sing theme songs from childhood shows, and feel like we would never know such tenderness, such camaraderie, that we learned something profound about ourselves, and that we have grown so much older than we were a month before. We take photos, limbs entangled, hair down, guns pointing like an accessory, cigarettes like fireflies. The night deepens and tomorrow tugs at us, and we are fierce and buoyant and terribly young and on the brink of something grand and indefinite and bigger than us.

14

 D
O
Y
A
L
I

I
S
L
A
M

Doyali Islam

Doyali Islam's second poetry book is *heft* (McClelland & Stewart, 2019). Her poems have been published in *Kenyon Review Online* and *Best Canadian Poetry*, and she serves as Poetry Editor for *Arc*. In 2017, Doyali was interviewed on CBC Radio's The Sunday Edition and was a National Magazine Award finalist.

she

for la famille faisons

I

she is a stern woman whose cheeks rarely betray
a fissured smile. she followed
her merry brown-beard of a husband
into apex'd wilderness, forgoing parisian perfumes
for the perfume of the woods—çitronelle;
and she adds her own cigarette puff to the smoke
of the log-burning stove.
she won't let me sit down at the counter
to chop the white cabbage fine—no
meat, no dairy; ! is she even french?
her mantra:
je fais; je pense pas; je fais.

2

he built their abode over eight years
in the talon-grip of the mountains
stone
by
stone
amidst les hortis stinging and
the troop of beady-eyed, calculating goats ringing
their collar bells past the front door.

3

i once made an accidental pact
upon those nettles, palm down, five fingers, all,
more scathing and reddening than pledging
in a court of law.
marches since, i have traversed sideways streets,
silver-slipper'd feet, ankles quick to dance
over pavement, easy glide without wet
boots or an obstinate donkey holding my place
while he chomped the gruff slope and made me wait,
as if he were a roman commander.
my mantra:
allez, çaesar; allez!

4

they yet live out seasons, held by unseen forces,
with children, three, whose maman is pyrénée
rock, wed to a papa of comic relief.
they caress the land in all its moods, harsh tricks,
and abatements, just as the big river
(whose uncompromising freeze once bathed
my naiad limbs) does, clinging, flashing
past, and mating with every rock unturned.

5

the land, they claim it as theirs, peg it
in conquest with three-sided outhouse, yellow-
tarp'd cabin, terraced garden, chèvrerie;
while a falcon prowls overhead, and
black ants march inside the breadbox, and
on the kitchen counter, claim undefended
blonvilliers brown sugar cubes as their own.

15

LESLIE SHIMOTAKAHARA

Leslie Shimotakahara

Leslie Shimotakahara holds a Ph.D. in English from Brown University. Her memoir, *The Reading List*, was winner of the Canada-Japan Literary Prize, and her fiction has been shortlisted for the KM Hunter Artist Award. She is the author of two novels, *After the Bloom* and *Red Oblivion*, published by Dundurn.

The Breakwater

Despite the scuffed bricks and boarded-up windows, the building maintained a certain air of elegance. It looked like a small, abandoned hotel. The ornamental mouldings on its façade worn flat with time. He remembered the odd hush of excitement he'd felt in his stomach, all those decades ago. Bags of freshly laundered linens heavy in his arms. Rosalind, the girl who would usually answer, had a cloud of auburn hair that accentuated the paleness of her skin, her delicate features. After taking the linens, she would reach into her pocket for some coins, and sometimes, if having a slow afternoon, she'd flirt and giggle melodiously.

A couple of times, Rosalind had even invited him inside, offering to give him his tip "in a different way." It had taken some effort for Mas to pull away from her light, coaxing touch—the laughter of more lovely creatures audible from the interior.

"What's the matter, Mr. Proper?" The air between them aswirl with her perfume. "Your brother, Sam, comes in all the time."

Crossing the street, Mas rejoined his daughter and her family.

"Dad, why were you staring at that building?" Wendy asked, pushing her large white sunglasses up, like a headband. Her eyes looked worried.

"It's just a place I remember from the old days."

When he failed to elaborate, Wendy sighed and looked down at the map of Victoria she always had in hand, folded into a long rectangle. "Anything else on Store Street you want to see?"

He shook his head. They'd already stopped outside the small apartment where Mas had lived with his five siblings, before the war. From the sidewalk, the second-floor window looked just as dingy as he'd remembered. This whole stretch was pretty much a dump. Back in his day, at least it'd been inhabited. Now, there was hardly a soul to be seen anywhere, beyond the odd vagrant or junkie.

During the years they'd lived here, their father had died of a stroke. So Mas had had to drop out of high school to work at the dry-cleaning shop and support the family. Sam was only one year younger, so he could have done *something* to help out, too, couldn't he? But helping out had never been Sam's style. Drinking, gambling, whoring, and hanging out with the thugs who ran Chinatown, now that was Sam's style.

Although they looked remarkably similar—to the point that people had mistaken them as twins, when they'd been kids—the two brothers couldn't have been more different. Mas, short for Masao, the name that Japanese parents typically gave to their eldest son. It even meant something like "holy" or "righteous." Sam, on the other hand, had at the soonest opportunity ditched his real name, Osamu.

Mas, Sam. Each name the inverse of the other, like some despised mirror image you could never get away from.

"I'm starving, Grandpa," Lisa piped up. She was ten and it seemed that her whole life revolved around her next meal or snack. "Is it too early for lunch?"

"Didn't we just have breakfast an hour ago?"

Wendy ruffled her daughter's hair. "According to the map, Chinatown's just a few streets over."

"I could go for some dim sum," David said, patting the slight belly beginning to form beneath his red golf shirt.

"Me too, Daddy—shrimp dumplings!"

Lisa opened her little drawstring purse and put on a pair of sunglasses that were a smaller version of her mother's. They both had the same chin-length haircut too, the bangs lightly feathered. Cut by some fancy, overpaid hairdresser, no doubt.

"Sounds good," Wendy said. "And then maybe this afternoon, Dad, we can go to Butchart Gardens? Isn't that where there's a Japanese tea garden, where the Japanese community had picnics, before the war?"
"I very much doubt it's still there." The sun was suddenly bothering Mas's eyes.

"The government cleansed the city of all traces of us, *after we'd all been rounded up and thrown in camps.*"

Silence.

Well, good. Good for everyone to take a break from being so chipper. All this reminiscing and revisiting old places was getting to be exhausting. He didn't even know what the point was. Wendy had insisted that it would be good for him—good in some vague, unspecified way. And since he'd received the redress money last year, he could no longer claim that he couldn't afford the trip. (How shocked they'd all been when Mulroney had actually come through and paid every Japanese-Canadian, who'd been interned, twenty-one thousand dollars in compensation.) Still, it grated on Mas how his family was treating this like a vacation, expecting everyone to be in an upbeat mood. He wished that his wife was still alive; having her around would take some of the pressure off him, at least.

*

He was right about the Japanese tea garden being gone. Or it wasn't open, it was closed for rebuilding and replanting—some excuse like that. He doubted it would be as impressive as it used to be, anyway. As they wandered through the English and Italian gardens, past the explosions of roses in full bloom, Wendy made a sharp comment at some point about how his bad mood was starting to be infectious. A shawl of guilt settled over Mas's shoulders. But he couldn't shake the gloom off. It didn't matter whether they were cracking open lobsters or looking at paintings by Emily Carr or standing outside the Empress Hotel, where he'd worked as the doorman the year before war broke out. The mood kept spreading across his insides, like an indelible tea stain.

And then, to his surprise, over breakfast one morning, he found himself making a suggestion. Yes, there was one place he wouldn't mind visiting. A place he had fond memories of. So they got in the rental car, Mas giving directions, while David drove. The sky was overcast as they approached, hugging the shoreline. The greyness of the weather made the red base of the lighthouse, at the end of the breakwater, stand out all the more vibrantly, even from a distance. By the time they'd parked, the wind had picked up speed and it had started to rain. Mas suggested that they grab their umbrellas.

"Oh, I don't know," Wendy said. "It looks so far. What if the rain gets worse?"

Lisa also didn't seem keen on getting wet.

"Fine. I'll go by myself."

"Mind if I come with you?" David said.

The two men stepped out into the drizzle. Mas didn't even bother to take an umbrella; he wanted to feel the elements against his skin.

The place hadn't changed much at all. Massive pieces of driftwood piled on the boulders along the beach, snake-like coils of brown kelp floating just below the water's surface. Perhaps there was a bit more of it, these days. As they walked farther out, more ropes of dead kelp lay on the big cement blocks that lined both sides of the breakwater. You could still jump down there to fish. In fact, a couple of boys were there right now casting lines, their faces hidden behind dark hooded sweatshirts.

They were sitting exactly where Mas and Sam had once sat, just past the first bend where the water was semi-shallow. The trick was to let your lure hit the sandy bottom, then use an unhurried, jigging retrieve. Sam had taught Mas this technique. That had been when they were still boys—friends, almost—before everything had turned to shit. Sometimes, they would fish farther out, where the current was stronger and you might even hook a salmon.

"Did you ever fish when you were a kid?" Mas said. David was Japanese-American, from Oregon; there was probably good fishing out there, too.

"Can't say I did. My father wasn't really the fishing type. How about you?"
"Sure, I used to fish here, in fact. The lingcod I'd catch was ugly as anything, but it tasted all right, fried up in butter."

While continuing to stroll, they stared out at the sky, like a giant smoke cloud moving in slow motion.

"There's a famous sea monster I once glimpsed around here."

"Really?" David said, smiling. "What did it look like?"

"The head resembled a horse. It had giant fins that flapped around, creating a blur of shadows."

Sam was the one who'd first caught sight of the creature—a dark, amorphous thing in the distance. *Look! Look!* He'd cried out, as if it were a sign of luck that he'd been blessed with the sighting. Mas, on the other hand, hadn't been willing to trust his eyes. A part of him still thought it had all been an illusion. And even if the monster had been real, it certainly hadn't filled Mas with a feeling of good fortune. Just the opposite, in fact. A portent of trouble to come.

It wasn't as though he'd never thought about his brother, over the years. It wasn't as though Mas had set out to erase Sam from their lives—it'd just somehow happened. And maybe it was for the best that things had turned out this way. Sam had in many ways been spared: he hadn't been forced to live through the indignities of the internment, or the upheaval of being relocated to Ontario in the aftermath, or the endless stress of having to rebuild your life from nothing, with a wife and brood to support. Throughout all that, Sam had been safe, protected. A clean bed, clean clothes, three square meals a day. It probably hadn't been too bad at all. Mas pictured his brother in a fluffy, white bathrobe, flirting with all the nurses.

Then Mas looked down at his own hands, the knuckles arthritic and misshapen, the tip of the middle finger on the left reduced to a blunt stub—thanks to an accident at the old steel plant. Sometimes, the finger still ached. Not the tip, but the actual flesh that was missing. Phantom limb pain, the doctors called it.

That night, he couldn't sleep. The bed at the motel was lumpy. And then, it was too late to sleep anyway, faint dawn light filtering through the curtains, the smell of coffee wafting up from the diner below. Mas got dressed and went down to the reception desk, where a pert blond girl greeted him cheerily. Extracting from his wallet a slip of paper with an address, he hesitated for a moment, doubting she would even be able to help him. But after consulting a book of maps, she traced the route in red pen on a map for him. It would probably take about twenty minutes to drive there, she said.

At the little convenience store off the lobby, he bought *Reader's Digest* and *National Geographic*, as well as two chocolate bars and a cup of watery coffee. Sipping it, he sat on a wooden bench for the next hour and a half, the paper bag containing the magazines and candy clutched on his lap. At last, Wendy, David and Lisa came down looking for him.

It was their last day in Victoria; their flight back to Toronto would depart that evening. Mas passed the map to his daughter, while saying, trying to sound casual, "If we have time, I'd like to pay a visit."

"Acacia House. What is this place?"

"What does 'acacia' mean, Mommy?" Lisa peered down at the map, too.

"It's some kind of plant, I think." Wendy crinkled up between the eyebrows. "Why, Dad? Who lives there?"

"A relative ... A cousin. A distant cousin."

"Um, okay." She continued to look at him strangely.

During the drive, everyone was pretty quiet. Mas could sense the wheels of his daughter's brain turning.

"Dad, is this the cousin you used to send care packages to, each month? The magazines and candy bars?"
He remained silent. Years ago, when Wendy had been a teenager, she'd asked about the packages that she would see him wrapping in brown paper. He'd become flustered and snapped at her. Later, he'd worried that she might go poking around and ask one of her aunts about the recipient's identity. But if she had, his sisters had covered for him. After all, it was their secret to bear, too.

Leslie Shimotakahara 159

They hadn't had any choice, had they? So there was nothing to feel guilty about, was there? By the time Sam had turned to them for help, he was already too far gone. Oh sure, Mas had had some idea of what was happening—he couldn't claim to have been entirely blindsided. Although Sam hadn't lived with them for years, Mas would run into him from time to time on the street. Toward the end, he hadn't looked so good. Gone was the swagger of confidence, the flashy clothing. His old buddies, who ruled the gambling dens of Fan Tan Alley, had clearly deserted him. How Mas came to dread these run-ins. Sam would smile at him, with a limp wave, his eyes as vacant as rain puddles. Too many drunken, dope-fuelled nights had leached the life from him and a rusty rash had erupted around his mouth— the same rash that disfigured poor girls like Rosalind, after the brothels had used them up and thrown them in the gutter.

Everyone knew it was only a matter of time before syphilis made you turn funny in the head. When Sam showed up on their doorstep, one evening—as dishevelled as a hobo, begging to be let inside, claiming that gangsters were coming to kill him— Mas knew that his brother had gone crazy. There was no other way to put it.

They couldn't have a madman living in their tiny apartment. What would the neigh-bours say? And his sisters were all terrified of Sam—terrified of what Sam had become. So the next day, Mas didn't go to work. Guiding his brother by the elbow, Mas got him onto a ferry to the mainland, where there was a large, imposing hos-pital called Essondale. Everyone knew about Essondale. "It'll just be for a month or so," Mas whispered in his brother's ear, as they approached the dark, fortress-like building. "Just until the doctors can help you get better. And you'll be safe here— safe from the gangsters."

But a month turned into six months. Then the Japanese bombed Pearl Harbor, throwing everyone's lives into chaos. Mas didn't even get a chance to visit his brother before he and the rest of their family found themselves being carted off to internment camps.

Still, he'd done what he could, what little he could. No doubt, he should have acted sooner. Many years after the war had ended, Mas had written letters and made a string of phone calls to find out what had happened to Sam. Essondale had been renamed by then and the facility had been downsized. But Sam was still in the system. He'd been moved around quite a bit over the years and now was at Acacia House.

They were approaching the place right now, coming up the long driveway. To Mas's surprise, Acacia House actually looked like a house. A large, taupe Victorian, with a deep verandah. Although there were two wicker chairs outside, it didn't look like they got much use.

"You all better wait in the car," he said to his family.

Feeling like he wasn't quite in control of his legs, Mas made his way up the front steps and rang the doorbell. A girl dressed in pink scrubs answered. He explained who he was and asked to speak to Mrs. Marion Carter, the Director of Care; Mas had written to her, from time to time, over the years.

Mrs. Carter turned out to be a small, grey-haired woman with a kind, lined face; she appeared surprised to see him and not terribly pleased. "It's better if you tell us ahead of time that you're planning to visit, sir. It gives us time to prepare the individual."

"I'm sorry, but I'm flying home tonight."

With a sigh, Mrs. Carter led him into a nicely decorated living room— throw pillows on the flowered sofas, framed watercolours of gardens and beaches on the walls. A handful of old ladies in pastel cardigans dozed in their wheelchairs, in front of some soap opera. The place seemed quite civilized, far nicer than Essondale.

Mrs. Carter was gone for some time. And then Mas saw her slowly descending the staircase, with a man clutching her arm. It was Sam, his eyes downcast, fastened on his slippered feet. He was wearing the pale grey sweater from Marks & Spencer that Mas had sent two Christmases ago. He'd aged remarkably well, far better than Mas. Sam still had a full head of salt and pepper hair, and his skin was relatively unlined. In spite of everything, life had perhaps treated him all right, in the end. He'd been sheltered from life's struggles and heartbreaks. That was something, wasn't it? And surely, over the years, someone would have explained to him that his family hadn't abandoned him—or if they had, *it hadn't been that simple*. The war, the internment, the never-ending struggle to make ends meet. Marriage, three daughters to raise. A sickly, demanding mother, who'd lived with Mas until her dying breath.

"Sam, it's me." Mas rose from the sofa, something like hope cresting in his chest. By now, his brother had reached the base of the staircase.

Slowly, Sam looked up. For a moment, it was as though he were looking at a foggy reflection in the mirror, trying to discern some half-familiar semblance. Then, like a spooked horse, he backed up on his heels, frozen. While Mrs. Carter stroked his back, he stepped backward and stumbled on the step, all colour drained from his cheeks, his eyes squeezed shut.

So his brother didn't want to see him. Mas understood this fact, just as he understood that there was nothing he could ever do to reverse it. But they were still brothers, like flipsides of the same tarnished coin, and Mas would continue to send the care packages for the rest of his life.

16

C
H
A
R
L
E
S

C.

S
M
I
T
H

Charles C. Smith

charles c. smith has written and edited fourteen books. He studied poetry with William Packard at New York University, edited three collections of poetry and his poetry has appeared in numerous journals and magazines, including *Poetry Canada Review, the Quill and Quire, Descant, Dandelion, Fiddlehead.* His recent books include: *travelogue of the bereaved, whispers* (2014) and *destination out* (2018).

4 for julius eastman
(1940-90)

i – storyteller/griot

with what there is to know   and all that fits like stones

within memory   once unknown forgotten as if a dream

not wanting to be told   censured in grieving

remembered now as flames   reborn and roaming

the borders of new york   ithaca buffalo vienna

ballet classes piano stools   concert halls decked in black

the gay underground   village of subway washrooms

10 a.m. whiskey in a trench coat   rehearsals

in black leather and chains   on the lower east side—

your buffalo house   a white space open to many

you dropped things when there   clothes and lovers

the homeless man you invited in   who took you for a ride

those unpredictable notes   in your later improvised compositions

evil nigger stay on it prelude to st joan gay guerrilla—

that deep baritone   mad as a king a supplicant saint

defiant in a sinister all-consuming rage   fingers plowing pianos

and cellos groaning the weight   of spirit memories—

an anomaly   the music stuck to your skin

would not let you be   and carried you into oblivion

away from singleterry   and the brooklyn philharmonia

who matched your notes `   with some sense of belonging

quivering in a form that would not offer itself   nor set aside

provenance in a common hue   to any who could

easily be seen   and what that fueled you to do

once the forbidden tomes of sex and skin   let you loose like a knife

sharpened on the edge of disdain   your complete

and utter deliverance into what you did   and how—

and with whom?   and the terms you set for sharing? with

only a few following?   out of love? sex? disbelief?

angling like small children   held close then left astray—

but were you ever open enough   to let anything else in?
such lightning in stories   your music and imagination

your strange and sudden   arrivals departures
at the loading gate   of the ephemeral

the branding of a label   you would live to regret—

so instead of a sinecure   you sought out the 'sin to cure'
with little regard for anything   especially yourself

and those years you went missing   with none aware of your passing
until eight months after   a small capture in the 'voice'

reminding those who abandoned you   of your time and telling
the blistering hypnotic succulence   your voice and notes

dance and 10 cellos 8 hands   on four grand pianos—

it is this telling   your dark hang outs and hoods
the tumble turning falling alone   a wanderer wounded

cloistered into timelessness   a sodden mystery like no other
with so many before without sequence   and several coming after

you found the branch   it cracked through your telling

and you fell   black icarus without angel wings in america

ii – (african spirit)

you are our child   water spirit
bathed in brine and oil   sharing sweat

the beauty of our shadows   and their glow
in those secluded spaces   we know—

they say there were none   before you
what would they know   i come to speak our names

mati   malungo   malongue batiment   sippi mahu
tongzhi   igbo women staying british guns with spears

azandi quimbanda mzili   kitesha tinkonkana eshenga
mwanga and his baptized celibates   chanting death

they couldn't   wouldn't see
our arms asleep in vespers   our members

pouring into openings   sublime and wet
tongues   without words washing

inside nights' belly on the hunt   beneath starlit

Charles C. Smith 169

leaves and the baobab's boughs   bent into wisdom—

on soft cloth our legs   our lips and fingers scathing
the echoing silence   of pleasure and tenderness

you gave all of yourself   as we did
then found ourselves alone   without comfort

on a journey across endless waters
coiled in chains   shanties and long fields

hiding our shadows   with our shame
our loins purloined   for production

under the sign of a wooden cross   ·   bearing a dead man
broken   and burying everything that did not kneel

iii (black being then)
it is thunder   how i want this clap in my ear
shango's tree-trunk   sexy black thighs

scaling mau mau mountains   earth-pounding
step-by-step   across a martyred 'jungle' space

such 'evil' shrouded in blackness   my balls
dancing below lips

i use the word 'nigger' this way   to describe

the past as future   its wax holding everything

in place   this world away i come from to you

disguised   bared in boats' bellies' darkness

our bodies   bearded into each other soft bone

foam and waves   an overwhelming deep

that cross of hunger   dangling atop stairs

a mirror on stone buildings   i entered

loathing such heightened   palaces of fear—

known as a child   stubborn and showing

my father moved on   this glimpse in his wandering eyes

i escaped into what i could not help but boldly blindly be

and speak to you now   from attica's darkest cell

dripping sweat and semen   spit and blood

the thugs and bullets   black sticks and gun fire

to stonewall's deepest cave's   passers-by flashing

Charles C. Smith   171

flashing towels in sweated saunas   seeking sex

then setting cage open   on stage
in buffalo   charring that master's red face—

i did what I did   and never once explained
only the moment mattered   its randomness bawdy and mad

and for this i was left   everywhere ahead yet behind
the white walls in front   my every breath and sound—

it was my will to contend   undefined definitive defamed
defrocked   and rocked into echoes of public washrooms

my scripts buried in trash   my ensembles bleeding like fleas
every nerve so purposefully   lewd loud-mouthed and open

a thirst between needles scotch   whisky
outside ivied university walls   feint with praise

until long after   my body returned some time ago
 like water   to the earth...

iv – (black being now)
i found his words

as if they were mine

this was not 'el cimarron'
that rebel of respect and decency

caught between the teeth of steel demons
held on screen in the master's stroke—

he did not want a veil as ceiling wall as bar
his body silenced like a thief

with blood pumping purple sparks
his heart in vast occult shade

arteries wide open
a trap he set for others caught him

breathing his own way
rumbling torment and fear

the agonies plagued upon his
bed sheets bath houses subway washrooms

a long way from ithaca buffalo rotting inside the apple

suckling a bottle somewhere in his coat pocket

markings notable up his sleeves

attica stonewall black bodies beneath police guns
and men unearthed in a toronto garden

his eyes mirroring windows
each day the blues of the rostrum

stops at his station the whistle blares
steam rises from the side of the tracks

this journey always beginning
never done

eastman was an openly gay black artist within the early days of american minimalism, passionate and openly political about who he was as a black queer and what that meant. these 4 poems are excerpts from a longer work in progress 'searching for eastman'. they are the voices of a storyteller/griot, an african spirit, a black being during the 1960s/70s and a black voice now.

going home

the long narrow island falls away behind thick green water
seagulls blanket the sky and circle a drab orange ferry
that moves like an ocelot slowly disengaging

out of the creaking wooden dock it slides into the open
where the seething atlantic eats the littered hudson
churned into mist by the old boat's propellers

small cargo tugs and rusting ocean freighters
lug huge loads like snails and turtles east and west
thick grey smoke inching from their black stacks

i have made this journey often and watched
the place where i grew fade into distance
saw again and again the thin white church spire

small offices of government and business give way
to busses climbing out of their stalls like ants
commuter trains' steel wheels screeching sparks

then receding quicker than the memory
of an alzheimer patient dwindling
behind yellow walls of a sanitorium

the crew calm as can be expected
they share cigarettes coffee curses bets
on these seemingly endless trips they make

while i am on another excursion
to la guardia airport for a short flight home
what i have done so many times over 26 years

several planes now fogged under military security
i lounge in departures for hours listening
to cnn's urgent news some imminent threat

a trump tweet replacing an o'brien on every tv screen
rebutting truths as if they were attack ads
complaining about what everyone else has

incursion

morning hangs on tips of green leaves
like gentle strokes of yellow paint
moved now and then by slow breezes—

out of a silence trembling in the east
a small brown hummingbird flies to its nest
and a brush fire wakes in the belly of the lake—

silver trout and green pickerel feel the restless heat
as sand crystals the coastline like stars
all day yearning for brilliance the desire of rest

in places where children rise to play
on swings in sandboxes on slides
they run across grass in and out of shadows

an eye perched for police cars
whose wheels cut damp brown spaces
with high speeds threatening sirens

scorching playground limits where death
hangs on the wrists of policemen like knock-off
rolex watches taken from those lying on the sand

by the quietly rippling waters of a deserted beach—

is this the magic?

imagine every moment   like this
sheer eccentricity   the charged air sings in the leaves
rain fades on rooftops   small dogs in the bush
play a rough percussion   beneath exposed trees—

nothing is imaginary   in the clouds' sharp bend
only the backs of the stars   and the height of trees—

nothing lends its weight   to the bleeding earth
or   hollows out its emptiness
like a faint orange skyline   fading into
a day when all else   fails memory—

then there is a shadow in the sky   mirroring earth
grey and tempestuous   sieged with its own demons—

there is a darkness as well   surrounding the break of evening
when the touch of a hand   casts stars into the rudderless void—

neither you nor i can make it here   something else
beyond compels what we   want so badly to do
with outstretched hands   burning into reason
and the inevitable journey   home to home—

it is all any can make of it   each moment

the next   and the next   (and the next)

the bright green glow   of a traffic light at rush hour

when everything goes   at unimaginable speeds

filtering sparks   in different directions

beneath a full white   november moon—

the passion of things

on certain evenings, the spirit simply leaves you. you then know solitude, like the hand of a child dangling on its own. in a playground, at the end of the day. where the circumference of fear sheds its universe. you can only imagine the anxiety. snow on the streets, the wind like a cold knife, the suffering you wanted to avoid. you remember waking, early sparks and smoke from the streets in the room, through a television set. what burned was hope, into blackness, you and so many others, found, fists tightened, teeth gritted, anger in the darkness. the everyday, the constant air. you are left to breath. and then the spirit left, unacknowledged. the hands that held it still, like a small flower in a bowl, floating in water, was no longer interested. your words, along with your own deep breaths, banished in the dim lit living room.

D
A
N
I
E
L
E

D'
O
N
O
R
I
O

Daniele D'Onorio

Daniele D'Onorio is a writer and performer of poetry, songs, plays, and prose. Born in a hospital atop a mountain edge in Veroli, a small city in south-central Italy, he grew up in Canada and lives in Brampton, Ontario. His writing evades genre and leaves few subjects untouched.

No Camp for the Soul

Churning Internment (an introduction)

Monday, June 10th of 1940 is widely remembered as another day Canadians thanked the heavens they weren't living in Europe. However, for a minority living within Canadian borders the thought may have actually been the opposite. For even though staying in Italy meant the rubble of war was quickly piling closer to home, you were still at home, and with your family. This wasn't the case for many Italians in Canada on the day lurking, mostly, in the shadows of Canadian history. In the months leading up to the 10th, many Italians were under the staked out gaze of the RCMP as files were compiled and regular surveillance was carried out on thousands of Italians and their businesses and cultural establishments. On that Monday morning RCMP officers sprung into action all over the country taking hundreds of men into custody, with little to no grounds, and putting thousands of others under tight and indefinite watch consisting of surprise visits, monthly check-ins, detailed activity reports, and heavily restricted mobility. Those taken from their families were sent to live, and carry out indentured labour, in one of three main internment camps in remote locations spread across Canada.

By now, if you're Italian, of Italian decent, or represent any racial or ethnic minority, you can probably feel your temperature rising and hands clinching tighter with every word. For many years, my feeling was often the same. But this wasn't written to conjure old wounds. Its aim is the very opposite, actually. This was written to initiate the healing we've all needed for longer than any of us can truly put our intellect on. Whether you knew of this history or not, you have been touched by it in ways you may not yet be aware of. If this work is your first contact, I am honoured to have introduced you to it. Presenting Italian internment the way I have chosen is for both those just stepping into this light and those who have forgotten the peace darkness can bring. There is much more to arriving at the body in the mirror than meets the eyes. The pride we feel for who we are now may have been what brought us to be it in the first place. And so, be grateful for your cultural identity, share the best it has to offer with all who are open to it, but remember that who you are culturally will never sum up who you are actually.

Song of Liberation

On the morning of June 10th in 1940, Italian men across Canada were taken from their families without warning in RCMP raids on their homes, jobs, and social safety nets. Nicco D'Brama was torn from an apartment lobby while peering into an empty mailbox on his first day off from work since arriving in Canada in the summer of 1938. His wife and three children all under the age of 10 never saw him again. The paper mill he worked at was never raided. After the latest installment of a yearlong spree of failed escape plans and break-ins of other internee's shacks, Nicco found himself in camp headquarters for a particularly aggressive disciplinary trip. While on this visit, Nicco catches a glimpse of a framed Oath of Citizenship on the wall of the camp director's office and spends a sleepless night wading through an ocean of visions he neither prompted nor knew how to explain. Days after this final disciplinary trip, once blood was mopped, breaths were caught, tables turned upright, and reports completed, what follows was found on the wall next to the oath:

I swear...

- we didn't willingly pack ourselves into cap-
tained tin cans headed for work the locals won't
do but gladly supervise, then get torn and quar-
tered for soldiering in a war we were running
from in the first place. I don't swear much at
all actually. When I do, it's less in promise
more in prowess. Mostly when I'm tired from a
long day in camp. English swearing has no heart,
in either use. When we swear we shake the heavens. These Canadians slap their knees. We kick
St. Peter's chair so hard it makes him question
his purity. We swear as a last resort. Not like
we hold our tongue until we are about to pass
out from anger, quite the opposite. More like
we know that because our swearing is so se-
verely damning the moment it drops from our lips
and races sweat beads to the floor, we are ready
to face Leopold levels of karma just so we can
have our moment. It's a burden and a bounty but
always better than pledging allegiance. Who's
folded whites don't stink of bleach anyway?

That I will be faithful...

- to whatever gets me through this hell they've
put together for us to fade away in. It won't be
some human though. This can't be left to anyone
with anything to gain from pain. So recognizing

God in everything has become a pastime for time I wish would pass faster. Blind faith is the only kind challenged by ego. I heard this in a dream once while smudging with my past. The past is the only kindling we need to ignite dreams of the future. Faith is when you no longer allow your ego to keep you from the message. The last couple of years have been hard but faith still wakes us up in the morning and I brush my teeth wondering if it's the real kind. I wonder how much we'll have to ask of it? How far will we be pushed? How much deeper will they ask us to dig? How many of us will run out of earth to withdraw before we discover our lack of deposits in the past has delivered us to this present? When did faith fall so far from our minds we reach through a familiar arsonist's flames for a chance to kiss charred lips and resuscitate blackened lungs?

And bear true allegiance...

- to who? Who walking the earth right now is worthy of such a thing as true allegiance? And whose allegiance is pure enough to offer to a being that worthy? It's a matter of escaping a prison without walls and a quick sand floor. We will make great efforts at what seems easy but most will choke on pork while antirhythmically wading naked through Monsanto lotus fields. For some walking slowly is allowing us to bear full detailed and calculated witness to each inch disappearing. While other's panicked clutching and aggressive treading is accelerating a slow death. Funny how time passes without question yet still allows us to respond with action on a secret choice affecting every moment. If I bear anything in what remains of this life, it will be honesty to that choice and humility for the outcome.

And bear true allegiance...

- to who? Who walking the earth right now is worthy of such a thing as true allegiance? And whose allegiance is pure enough to offer to a being that worthy? It's a matter of escaping a prison without walls and a quick sand floor. We will make great efforts at what seems easy but most will choke on pork while antirhythmically wading naked through Monsanto lotus fields. For some walking slowly is allowing us to bear full detailed and calculated witness to each inch disappearing. While other's panicked clutching and aggressive treading is accelerating a slow death. Funny how time passes without question yet still allows us to respond with action on a secret choice affecting every moment. If I bear anything in what remains of this life, it will be honesty to that choice and humility for the outcome.

To Her Majesty Queen Elizabeth the Second...

- whom I may never meet but will come to know me through the dot-line-line-dot, dot-line, dot-dot, line dot howling and reverberating through the ether, I pledge to be heard: each beat will jolt you from sleep. rob your first three wak-ing breaths, daily. paint your forehead with the graze of an arctic spear. And as you grip to resettle the dust you hold so dear, your palms will commune with particles of discarded cos-tumes. few you pressed regularly against your chest and covered with the breath that proceeds vows of attachment, many you folded careful-ly so your crest lay over the forehead, others you left unshod to show the world just how far you will go to secure the treasures promised to you by asthmatic inspiration. the bounty of your birth is a mirage. you are but a Moretus peak reaching out for the Pacific. you were not giv-en forty days and so will be left to wander much longer until you learn to swim with renunciation

or are purified by drowning. I write this in re-
covery, recognizing pain.

My wife and three children have become dead to
me so I don't wrap my remaining thoughts around
the tree of their despair watching each day fall
as they decay in the cold wind following my dis-
appearance.

Queen of Canada...

- *is a chalice filled with the blood of wandering
heartless soldiers and polished with the sour
wine of the drama. An eternity of acid rainy
seasons won't erase the dripped trail up the
castle steps leading back to your iron thrown.
The best you will claim is prominence and patina, nothing more. Only the pain of my settling
karmas could push me to the clarity with which
I can now see past myself, and into you. I no
longer pray, so I have little to offer you other
than love, and this reminder: your responsibil-
ity for moving a piece on the board is equal to
that of knocking one over with your reach. It's
a strange twist of fate I am the outsider that
would be chosen to reveal Canada will never be
free in your arms. But then, maybe that's how
you wish it. You will continue to push your beliefs and your language. But the hollering you*

allow those you welcome into your chain-linked
embrace will never reverberate like the silence
and independent self-sovereignty of freedom.
Limit the energy you put into this hold for the
forthcoming storm will require every glint.

Her Heirs and Successors...

- have not arrived, and will not make future arrivals, at their circumstances by accident. We
all ignite bodies manifested in times and places
preordained by every pen stroke and paint splatter. For even scribbles in the margins are part
of the script, some articulate more than bullets through the soft palate, lingering glanc-
es, or ravaged screams in the dark. Every step
has made us heirs of our particular fortunes and
successors of who we once appeared to be. A num-
bered dollar lifted in the shadows, a path left
clear long before needed, a window reduced to
shards falling too slow to catch dust of running
feet, a body pulled to the surface just in time
to keep it occupied, a heart allowed to tumble
down freshly painted stairs as it rested into
one sided trust, a mistake claimed and placed in
the light, a flower eyed but never gifted, a good
night's sleep shared with the tormented, a stamp
placed too close to the edge, a lie dressed but

never played, a letter written in anger and
forgotten in the fire. Only a lack of discern-
ment can allow you to miss the meaning of each
movement. This is true, no matter whom you have
come to, so find a blade, a flame, and a thread-
ing needle. Get to work finding the difference
between cords you've coiled in remembrance and
cords you've allowed to fray. Aware of the un-
controllable laughter some of you will succumb
to, this gross echo is not far behind: the seat
you have inherited will only be as comfortable
as your consciousness allows. There is blood
dripping from the armrests, muffled by the many
books on your walls. Can you still hear droplets hitting the floor? We are all born unpredictable. Settling for that would be a waste,
but not surprising.

And that I will faithfully observe...
- the one law. Let us remain married to the faith
  that we are accountable for everything that
  happens to us in this place. Let this accountability run solely on love and respect for our
  every feeling, thought, and action for they
  will forever be shaping who we have been, who
  we are, and who we have yet to become. Our
  faith is not meant for surrender to anything

less.

The laws of Canada...

- were written in ignorance of the one law. A
legless life is a common prescription for any
being taking a sickle to the innate in order to sustain the acquired. In this swing or
the next, or the thirty-second thousandth, the
blade will come around. Consider every word
here a call to come in from the field. I wonder
how many have checked how far they've strayed
from home?

   These laws have been written only for those
who may one day be in a position to wield the
pen for their own benefit. And their favour for
this privilege will grow until the lines between blood and ink are blurred and the vam-
pires walk chin up in the daylight.

And fulfil my duties...

- *day after day, hiding under Jacobs ladder re-
citing the secrets in Daniel's verses till
caught and beaten for whispering too loudly.
It's now clear in how few of these days a vacant place remains for me. So each one is handled with care in constant practice while re-
linquishing fear of resembling a mere obedient*

wop. I rise earlier than expected to sharpen
the pick, listen to the wind guiding my swing,
study the ground, and do the work of expansion
on behalf of the sky.

As a Canadian citizen...

- ask why decay was chosen to represent you. When
has the colour red made someone like you think
of fertility, love, rebirth, strength, glory,
or freedom? In one eye, I see red very differently than even eight hours ago. In the other,
I see it as you still do. As you may be obligated to see it in perpetuity. Do you feel like
you are decaying? Is there a forgotten gust
your spine has yet to release? Has some rogue
humidity pooled in your subconscious? What
musty guilt blocks the ritual inhalation your
healing is hinged on? What are you hanging on
to, determined to drag through the snow across
haunted plains? Being someone who will never be
called a Canadian, offers of suffering that go
with such a title remain foreign to me. But no
one walks through the train station untouched.
This cancerian colony has revealed its tight
grasp on everything it declared itself to have
enthusiastically renounced. But pressure either brings reluctant eruption or shakes the

earth to reveal grand staff watermarks of care-
lessness. Either way, notice goes unheeded.
This cancerian colony lives in private judgment. Pointing out and condemning atrocities
and wrongs with every other word, only to har-
monize with them through dinner table shouting
and checkout line whispers. In smaller doses,
for twice as long, while sitting on the seed of
apologetic smiles, overgrowing to shade guilt
and cover the root of the problem.

Who has performed actions that would shape feet
gifted to dance with such a subtle force? If
you've gotten this far, who else but you could
find the restorative and benevolent cadence in
a storm capable of delivering a reset blink
of excruciating discomfort? These feet could
never find the downbeat long before they were
crippled. Instead, this voice has been chosen
to sing dance floors into existence for you to
come alive upon. Now let us count to the tempo
of liberation and step, strut, and stride ourselves into immortality among the stars.

Alessandra Naccarato

Alessandra Naccarato is an editor and award winning writer based on Salt Spring Island. Her work has received the Bronwen Wallace Award, been shortlisted for the CBC Poetry Prize and *Event Magazine*'s Creative Non Fiction Prize. She has toured nationally and internationally as a spoken word poet and worked with hundreds of emerging writers across the country.

Girlhood

I was a girl trying to start a fire with a magnifying glass;
I knew the names of things.
Then my body began towering itself towards god.
I became an archway, a hinge, a public institution.

There was no language in the architecture,
only the swinging of the door and my mother's warning,
rocks thrown in a deep river. I built myself a silence,
a raft. Cowered and ran, played dead

in the water where my mother's stones rested.
What I had was a name, given
to me by an aunt whose kidneys were failing.
With this I tried to fashion a deed to the house of my body.

All the windows were open, the doors unlocked.
In the living room, a girl with cut glass in her mouth.
In the bedroom, something I couldn't unsee.
So I took scarves from the mirrors until the walls

flooded with light. Wrote my name in ash, through water,
until it was clean. Bees swarmed from the mouth
of creation, the jaw of my dress. Around me, demolition:
thin light through a circle, and the blue smoke of grass.

The Fish

The story is he gives me a fish.

The problem is my hands only hold so much water.

The problem is my hands leak water.

The problem is I want it to keep living.

The setting is a municipal campground.

The setting is not far from the creek.

The setting is Thursday. A muggy, wet evening.

The smell of burning pine.

We turn away from the fire together.

We walk to his tent where the light is slanted.

This is where he gives me the fish.

This is where I can't unhold it.

The story is he's drunk.

The story is his father.

The story is my body should give it shelter.

The body rarely does what it's told.

The problem is I want to keep living.

The problem is my hands are not ponds.

The problem is he wants me to keep it.

The story is I give it back to the land.

This Is How You Make a Haunting

It takes three days to panhandle
enough for the bus, and then
your father is already on the shelf
our people use for the dead.

The cat's tail curled around
zucchini stalks, garden purring.
All earthworm and yellow flower, wet
as the day you left home.

Here is the bed. Here is
your tag on the milk store wall: *Mano
Negro*. Here is your long-haired brother
lifting the cat from the earth.

Hot oil in the pan. Fat mother
at the stove, battering flowers. Seven
years of black cloth, says she'll learn
the language now. Gives you

the wool inheritance — here you are
in his coat, thin and shot
full of junk, black-eyed eldest.

The rock wall leans onto

the highway, you hear the dead river
under your house. Two years
doesn't change the land,

just the body. Where a thorn
pierced your forearm, button your
father's sleeve. Visit the mausoleum,
its damp, sweet quiet.

Your name on the door, the blood
inheritance. Put your hand to
the language: here is your body,
here is your way to grow up.

There's a line in you still, three
children. I'll be that same body,
heaving at the flower's bright stem,

will need to know how cold
the stone was when you touched it.

How you vomited beside the plot,
shook for days in your room.

Mother skinning rabbits for soup,
brother holding a spoon of broth
to your small blue mouth.

Homestead

We borrowed a farm house and grew a glory of armpit hair.

Yard high with yarrow, thigh high with silk, uninvited to the wedding

down the road. What they'd call peculiar, at the punch bowl,

gas station. Queer as unbelonging. Queer as the oak leans

and moss invites itself in. We left the city without a driver's license.

The roof full of crows. A hive, a coop, a barrel of rain.

Slow dancing between appetizers with my hand on your silk.

They ask us politely to leave. Queer as in trespass. As in *all*

of god's creatures. Outside, you can hear a goat opening a universe.

My sister's hands on Pluto, turning. There is a black hole thrumming

in a high school, in a drug store nearby. Nobody gets out

of themselves alive. We look to Venus, count names we can touch.

Poplar, bullrush, homestead. Crescent, willow, dyke. You don't get

to take it with you, the sign reads: you might as well dance now.

J
A
E
L

R
I
C
H
A
R
D
S
O
N

Jael Richardson

Jael Richardson is the author of *The Stone Thrower: A Daughter's Lesson, a Father's Life*, a memoir based on her relationship with her father, CFL quarterback Chuck Ealey. *The Stone Thrower* was adapted into a children's book in 2016 and was shortlisted for a Canadian picture book award. Richardson is a book columnist and guest host on CBC's q. She holds an MFA in Creative Writing from the University of Guelph and lives in Brampton, Ontario where she founded and serves as the Artistic Director for the Festival of Literary Diversity (FOLD) which received the 2019 Freedom to Read Award from The Writers' Union of Canada. Her debut novel, *Gutter Child*, is coming January 2021 with HarperCollins Canada.

Resurrection Sunday

It had been two years since Emmanuel Bible Chapel had a lead pastor —two years of retired men with thinning hair and a pension for old testament apologetics sermonizing on stopovers in Mulberry Hills. Church members were leaving at a rapid rate, promising to come back when things were more stable, but the stalwart members of the little white chapel knew that the situation was dire. The congregation was in desperate need of a miracle. And, amen, the Lord answered.

Dale Williams—the only applicant in two years—secured the position after a phone interview with members of the pastoral search committee, which was headed by James Hawthorne and his spindly wife Anna-Lee. The couple believed that Dale Williams had a strong resume, a kind disposition and an incomparable knowledge of the Bible—a glowing review from EBC's most influential couple. And the rest of the committee wisely agreed.

James Hawthorne owned a car dealership in Mulberry Hills which earned a pretty penny, and his tithes single-handedly kept EBC in the black, with annual contributions so significant they had never been matched by the congregation's collective annual giving even before the exodus began—a congregation comprised mostly of dealership employees, correctional workers, and hard-working, salt-of-the-earth farmers. Whenever she got the chance, Mrs. Anna-Lee Hawthorne would tell anyone within earshot that James *insisted* on giving far above the Biblical ten-percent tithe, so that every member of the Mulberry Hills congregation was aware that the Hawthornes—on some fundamental level—

practically *owned* the small chapel in Mulberry Hills.

When the decision was made to hire Dale Williams, Sydney Mulligan —the third member of the pastoral search committee—arranged a Skype conversation to deliver the good news in order that he might lay eyes on the new pastor himself and dispel any concerns that might delay the arrangement. And while the video had not worked due to a poor connection that was typical in Mulberry Hills, the audio had been clear, allowing Sydney—a recently widowed and retired police officer—to have a meaningful discussion with the soon-to-be-pastor of EBC. Sydney explained that while the Mulberry Hills Penitentiary was just down the road, the town itself was incredibly safe despite its reputation as a home for no-good convicts. He told Dale Williams that the penitentiary was mostly filled with drunks and gangsters and foreigners who came to "stir up trouble", folks who once captured were no threat to residents of Mulberry Hills and committed members of EBC.

"Your family is in good hands here," he said.

Sydney Mulligan bragged about the Women's Group at EBC—a group his late wife had started, which met once a week to bake or quilt. He spoke of the children's ministry which served nearly 20 kids each week, providing goldfish crackers for children, free of charge. In mentioning the work of the EBC children's ministry, Sydney hoped the new pastor would put in a word to his wife so she would come and lead the ministry, continuing the good work of previous pastor's wives at EBC. Sydney believed that when you hire a pastor, you hire his wife as well—even if she never appears on payroll. Her crown was in heaven, after all.

Sydney's only concern after he got off the phone with the soon-to-be pastor of Emmanuel Bible Chapel was that according to the picture on the pastor's Skype profile, Pastor Dale William's wife was *black*—a word he conveyed to the rest of the committee with a mixture of surprise and concern. "While I'm entirely okay with this kind of thing," he said. "I think it's worth mentioning."

There was a thick pause, as though no one knew quite what to say to this, and it was Anna-Lee Hawthorne who chimed in first. "Well, perhaps Mrs. Williams will be able to offer new and interesting recipes for the Women's Group events," she said. "I have always wanted to make a good jerk chicken."

At this, James Hawthorne and the two other men on the committee shrugged, mostly out a desire for this two year search to finally be done.

But the person who was most excited for Pastor Dale Williams to arrive was Miss Haley Johnston. Haley had been the EBC secretary for nearly twenty years. She had been keeping the entire ship afloat—like Noah and the ark— since Pastor Holten Powell's unexpected death. She handled the budget and organized visiting pastors. And while she was incredibly capable, she had gained more than one hundred pounds these past two years by way of a stash of chocolates she kept in her desk and a nighttime pattern of eating five buttered slices of white Wonder Bread before bed. Thank God, for Pastor Williams ,she said to herself on the first Good Friday in a long time that actually felt *good*.

*

On Easter Sunday, Haley Johnston was sitting at the front desk awaiting the arrival of the new pastor when a thick-bodied black woman entered the office in a dress the color of the grape juice they watered down for communion. Haley stared up at the woman, wondering if she was on her way to one of those conjugal visits at the penitentiary and found herself lost. "May I help you?"

"You must be Ms. Johnston," the woman said. She had a deep and raspy voice, the kind Haley imagined singing soulful blues in dark, smoky places like the Dive—the Mulberry Hills bar Haley had heard about but never frequented having lived her entire life in the town devoted to God and free of unsavoury vices like cigarettes and alcohol and drunks.

"Can I help you?"

"I'm Dale Williams."

Haley Johnston sat there for a moment, stunned silent. "Dale...Williams?"

It was at that very moment that the final member of the pastoral search team, Mr. Timothy King, stepped into the office. Timothy King was the volunteer associate pastor and filled in as needed, speaking regularly from the Sunday pulpit while holding a job as a teacher at the local high school—a true teacher in every sense of the word, a teacher exhausted by the two jobs and his six kids. "Haley, let me know when Pastor Williams is here," he said.

Dale smiled at the man and then at Haley, waiting like the disciples at the transfiguration for a proper introduction. But Haley could hardly put words together, let alone sentences.

"Timothy...Pastor King, this *is*...Dale...Williams...Pastor...Pastor," she said, gesturing at Dale Williams then back at Timothy King, unsure and helpless. And the two desperate congregants prayed for a miracle.

*

A large crowd gathered to witness the reveal of Emmanuel Bible Chapel's new lead pastor and to celebrate the risen Lord on a warm Easter Sunday ushered in by a sign on the church lawn that read "Welcome Pastor Dale Williams" and "He is Risen"—announcements that ushered in excited residents of Mulberry Hills in equal measure.

James Hawthorne took his wife's hand and the pair climbed the small flight of stairs to begin the service, giving the entire congregation a much better view of Anna-Lee's impressive new shoes and matching Easter bonnet as she stood a few steps back from her husband, glowing as he introduced Pastor Dale Williams.

"Pastor Dale has three grown children, a daughter who has become a doctor, a son who teaches English, and another son who is serving our country overseas," he said.

The congregation smiled and collectively sighed, full of wonder, and James Hawthorne continued, his chest swelling with pride.

"Pastor Williams has served as the head of a Bible College and speaks three different languages. As a family, they have even adopted a refugee from Rwanda."

With every word, the congregation became more enthralled, fell more in love, and felt more convinced that this pastor, this find, was a true act of God. They had been faithful to the end and now they would reap rich rewards.

"Please rise and join me in welcoming Pastor Dale Williams to Emmanuel Bible Chapel," James Hawthorne said, concluding his introduction with a raised voice and just enough dramatic pause.

Eighteen rows of Easter Sunday churchgoers stood and leaned forward abruptly, hands clapped in applause, necks cranked to get a better view—everyone, that is, except Haley Johnston and Timothy King, who stood far more slowly, eyes closed as though in prayer.

Upon seeing the purple-clad woman, Anna-Lee Hawthorne's first thought was that of scorn and disapproval, mostly over her wardrobe—a fabric quality reeking of costs that seemed excessive and must be second-hand. But James Hawthorne was perplexed on a much more basic level. Who is that, he wondered.

Retired detective Sydney Mulligan recognized the woman from the profile photo right away, and while the rest of the congregation paused and murmured, their faces riddled with offense or confusion, he stepped on stage with an air of calm, placing his hand on Dale Williams shoulder, leaning in close and whispering, so as not to be heard. But the microphone at the pulpit was a new model the Hawthorne's had purchased with powerful range that ensured everyone in the sanctuary could hear clearly: "I thought Pastor Williams said the family wouldn't be joining us for another week."

"That's correct, Mr. Mulligan," Dale Williams said with an unaffected grin., volume clear and strong. "My family will not be joining me for another week."

With that, Dale Williams hands clasped her hands over the pulpit, standing with a confidence and patience that the pastoral search committee and everyone in the sanctuary sat down. "Thank you so much, Mr. Hawthrone, for that wonderful introduction," she said with a toothy smile. "It's an honour to be the new pastor at Emmanuel Bible Chapel. What a lovely town."

At these words—*It's an honour to be the new pastor*—the Hawthornes and Sydney Mulligan practically lost a breath—their bodies frozen still. It wasn't until Dale Williams petitioned the audience to bow their heads in prayer and spouted words of thanksgiving to God, to the church, to the selection committee, to Jesus for his immeasurable sacrifice, that the selection committee leaned forward in the front pew and began to whisper.

"How did this happen?" Anna-Lee seethed.

"I knew we should be concerned," Sydney seethed. "There was something about that woman I didn't trust. I could tell just from the photo."

By the time Dale Williams lifted her head with a purposeful amen, Mr. and Mrs. Hawthorne had made a decision. They stood and marched down the center aisle, followed by Haley Johnston and Timothy King, his doting wife and six children.

Five minutes later—after checking their mobile phones, which they clutched tighter than their Bibles—more churchgoers scattered throughout the church departed—all of whom were employees at the Hawthorne car dealership.

And as Pastor Williams' sermon delved into the life of Jesus Christ post-cruci-fixion, one by one, more members of the small congregation slipped out of the stoic sanctuary, sensing the disapproval of those departed and pressured by the glares of Sydney Mulligan, who hovered around the edges of the sanctuary nodding towards the back doors, so that by the time the sermon ended, only five people remained in the eighteen pews of Emmanuel Bible Chapel on Easter Sunday.

Jean Connor, an old woman whose eyesight had all but left, sat in the front row, unsure of what might happen if she left. Her walker was leaning against the wall, and despite the emptying of the room, despite the fact that she knew the church like the back of her hand and sensed an air of disapproval, she could not get over the strong timber of the new pastor's voice. So she nodded and listened and smiled as the pastor spoke of the faith of Mary Magdalene, a character she had always loved.

"Perhaps you, like Mary Magdalene, have felt overlooked and undeserving," Dale Williams said.

A man who had strolled in off the street wearing torn jeans and a brown faded t-shirt that read "Cool Beans" remained to the end as well, shouting through-out the sermon: "Amen, Sister, Amen", reminded of his grandmother who was a born rebel at heart. Each time he shouted praise, Dale Williams smiled and paused, a smile the Cool Beans man returned, having never been acknowledged in that way by someone so important, having felt truly seen for the first time in years.

But it was the trio who stayed to the end that touched Dale Williams most.

In the back of the church, a mother sat with two pre-teen daughters. They had long black hair and they stared up at Dale Williams as though she herself was a saint or an angel, as though every word was from God himself, just for them. "Do not grow weary. You are important to God," she said, as light streamed through the stain glassed windows like a sign straight from heaven.

The threesome attended EBC only occasionally, mostly on holidays. They lived across the road in a mobile home that hadn't moved in two years, awaiting the girls' father's release from the penitentiary. But they had never offered to help with the children's program or shown up for quilting, so the members of the congregation hardly paid them any mind. Anna-Lee Hawthorne had once offered to help the woman and the girls get away, to move somewhere safe, certain that the father must be an utter lowlife. But the woman with the long dark hair had declined the offer with an expression that looked to Anna-Lee like contempt.

"You can't force people to help themselves," she had sighed to her husband, having done all she could.

"Jesus loved women. He spent time with them, and he cared about them, in a way that even his own disciples didn't understand," Dale Williams said.

The women and the two girls stared and listened, enraptured, and when the sermon ended, the girls looked up at their mother and their mother looked down at them as though all three had felt a touch of something from outside this world.

But Sydney Mulligan headed onto the stage and walked Dale William out of the church, barely allowing her to shake hands with Jean Connor and Cool Beans, his hand pressed against her back with just enough force to alert her of expectations as she hugged the woman and the two girls tightly for far too long.

"That's quite a thing you did," Sydney murmured as he led her to the only car in the parking lot he did not recognize, the only car that could be hers —a small, nondescript white Toyota.

"Did you enjoy the sermon, Mr. Mulligan?"

Sydney Mulligan's jaw tensed because he hadn't thought about the sermon at all. He was too busy managing the mess she had made on a day meant to remind congregants of God's great mercy, a day wasted on what he now knew to be the careful work of a con artist.

"You should have told us," he said.

But when he looked down at Dale Williams, when he watched her climb into the front seat and wipe the dust from her shoes, he thought he saw her swipe away a tear before giving a small wave in the general direction of Emmanuel Bible Chapel and driving down the road out of town.

D
W
A
Y
N
E

M
O
R
G
A
N

Dwayne Morgan

Affectionately known as the Godfather of Canadian Spoken Word, Dwayne Morgan has shared his work on stages around the globe since 1993. The author of ten titles and eight albums, Morgan has also been inducted in to the Walk of Fame, in his hometown of Scarborough, Ontario.

Colin K

In 2016,

In response to injustice,

And police brutality,

San Francisco 49ers QB,

Colin Kaepernick,

Decided to take a knee,

Refusing to stand,

For the playing of the American Anthem,

Whose ideals,

Weren't living up to the experiences

Of those who looked just like him.

Imagine,

A people up in arms,

Because a black man chooses to kneel,

In order to take a stand,

For those,

Killed with their arms up,

put down like sick pets,

Just without the dignity.

This,

They considered disrespectful to the country;

More so than marches for equality,

Still happening in 2017,

More so than sports teams,

Named the Braves, Redskins, and Blackhawks,

More so than the thirty million dollars

That Lebron James makes,

But still comes home to find,

Nigger spray painted

On his front gate.

Clearly, Colin forgot

That signing a contract means,

Stepping away from your community,

And pledging allegiance to the league,

Whose owners sit like overseers,

Watching Black men

Make them money on their fields.

This feels all too familiar,

Almost like dé jà vu;

Don't worry about the others,

Be happy that they aren't you,

Don't notice the lynchings,

Even though they're in plain view.

Do what we pay you to do,

And don't worry about them,

Play your position,

So that you won't be next.

He, stepped offside,

And spent the season

On the bench.

2017,

and he still has no team,

possibly the end

of a life long dream,

simply for taking a knee,

to take a stand,

to speak for the voiceless,

from Mike Brown to Sandra Bland.

This is what happens,

When we refuse to be quiet.

This is what happens to those

Who disrupt and riot.

This is what happens

When we speak on injustice and violence,

In a world that would prefer us

To just sit and be silent,

Whether in sports, corporate America,

Or the spoken word;

Life just seems so much more comfortable,

When we are seen and not heard.

Teams that would benefit

From his talent,

See him as too much of a risk,

We're pretty safe when we're handling a ball,

But no-one wants a black man

Who stands up for shit.

That might affect the sale of tickets,

And people's enjoyment of the game.

Can you imagine,

If he inspired other athletes

To start doing the same,

To use their money and celebrity

To advocate for change,

But instead,

They make him an example,

His career is almost dead,

Because even unarmed and on our knees,

We still remain a threat.

Smile

I don't remember what I was looking for,
When I came across an old picture of me;
Blue plaid shirt,
Maybe twelve or thirteen,
Smiling from cheek to cheek.

Anyone who knows me,
Knows that I don't smile like that,
Anymore.
I wondered if I'd ever mourned that inner child.

I sat there, wanting to cry,
Unable to identify what had died inside.

I remember the scent
Of young love in bloom;
A botanical garden of possibilities,
Maybe twenty-two, twenty-three,
Twenty-one questions each night,
Conversations until sunlight,
Hoping that things will grow;
Wanting to know,
What makes each other tick,
Picking brains like flowers,

Wanting to know how our present

Was affected by our pasts,

Our upbringings, spiritual beliefs,

Life after the split between

My mom and my dad,

What impact their divorce had,

But I felt nothing like that.

I remember the fear of becoming a father

To my own seed,

Maybe thirty-two, thirty-three,

Wanting to be the best dad that I could be.

I remember our little family falling apart,

And how it felt like I was playing a part

In a play that I wanted no part of.

I remember holding you in my arms,

And how you'd scream

at the top of your lungs for your mom,

and she would tell me,

not to take it personally,

assure me that this was just a phase,

but words never erased the rejection and pain.

I remember the rain,

Maybe forty-two, forty-three,
And the heart ache of a new flame,
Wanting to flicker out,
Unsure of what this feeling was all about.

I mean,
Love brings both joy and pain,
And you can't force one to stay.

I remembered twelve, thirteen,
My father's decision to leave;
Feeling unloved, unwanted, abandoned.

I sat there, forty-two, forty-three,
Feeling unloved and unwanted.

I remembered thirty-two, thirty-three,
Feeling rejected by my own seed;
Twenty-two, twenty-three,
Lies so deep,
That I believed them to be true,
And then I remembered you,
Your unconditional love,
the smile that adorns your face,
and how I'd do anything to keep it in place.

Hard to believe

That it took thirty years to realize

The effects of my father's leaving;

My need to be loved, wanted, and accepted.

When I too, chose to leave,

I made sure to only place clothes in my bag,

Promising to do everything to keep your smile intact.

Even when your mom,

Works my last nerve,

I remember, and remind myself

That you deserve to smile,

And I sacrifice my ego,

To watch your cheeks raise,

And light up your face.

Some days,

I tell you that I love you,

And you don't say it back;

Too young to know the weight of words

That I never heard,

But time has taught me not to take it personally.

At forty-two, forthy-three,

I look at pictures,

And wish that I could smile,

Like I did at twelve, thirteen.

It might be too late for me,

So I live vicariously,

Remembering all that I lost as a child,

Every time,

Your cheeks raise,

And you brighten my world,

With your smile.

Facebook

I'm not on Facebook much these days. I'm amazed by the number of names that I know, of Black people that I've never met; the number of RIP's I've offered up, with the ease of status updates, and I don't want to get desensitized to the executions, but it seems like I'm frozen in place, stuck in a perpetual Groundhog's day, scrolling my feed, only to see the same damn thing; another innocent Black man killed.

So, I'm not on Facebook much these days, because I find it hard to explain, the weight on my heart and spirit, watching replays, of Black lives being lost on video, knowing that every one existed in vain, and paid leave is the price of a Black life.

I find it hard to explain my difficulties falling asleep; news reports being replayed, but this time the face is me. It's like my entire community is suffering through PTSD, every time we scroll down our Facebook feed.

We are stuck in this society, where those whose job it is to serve and protect, believe that if a woman is dressed suggestively, she deserves what she gets; if you ask too many questions, you're resisting arrest, if you're Black, and you're male, shoot first, then ask next.

This system is a vice that will squeeze your life like a cock ring. They've got us out in the streets screaming for justice with no Johnnie Cochran. The glove doesn't fit, but we always fit the description. America is sick, but doesn't even want a prescription; election coming, but silence from Trump and Clinton.

So what do these Black lives even mean? Maybe they only matter to me, matter to

Dwayne Morgan   229

we, as a matter of fact, if our symbol of justice is a woman wearing a blindfold, is it any surprise, that all that she sees is black?

I'm not on Facebook much these days, because I don't have it in me to deal with those who think that this is a joke, and don't know what it takes just for us to cope.

To be conscious of what it going on, is to put our sanity up for auction on a daily basis, and this feels all too familiar, so forgive me, if it takes me a while to re-spond to your messages, or you don't see me liking your posts. Right now, I'm just trying to take care of me, so I'm not on Facebook much anymore.

D
A
N
I
L
A

B
O
T
H
A

Danila Botha

Danila Botha is the author of two short story collections, *Got No Secrets*, and *For All the Men (and Some of the Women I've Known)* which was a finalist for the Trillium Book Award, The Vine Awards and The ReLit Award. She is also the author of the novel *Too Much on the Inside*, which won a Book Excellence Award and was short listed for a ReLit Award. Danila teaches creative writing at University of Toronto and Humber School for Writers.

Sometimes I Like to Shoot Kids

Yesterday morning I got to school forty-five minutes early only to find four kids having a fist fight. All I could see was tiny fists flying, and two boys lying on their backs outside my classroom. It was easier to identify them first, Liron and Maor. Liron was wearing his bright green t shirt and Maor was yelling. It took me a minute to realize what was happening.

Miryam and Jana, two tiny beautiful girls, were sitting on the chests, punching them. Jana even got a right hook to Maor's cheek. There was a part of me that hesitated to break it up. Liron and Maor were the kinds of pains in the asses that mercilessly mocked other students. The school was located on the second floor above a Pizza Hut, a grocery store and a Mcdonald's, and Liron spent his first recess whipping glass bottles at passing cars.

"What the hell do you think you're doing?" I asked him, trying my best to be some kind of authority figure.

He shrugged and looked at me. "Aiming for the windshield, Tamar."

I took a deep breath and got the principal. "I'm not cut out for this," I told her.

She shrugged. "You'll be fine. You've just been in America for too long. You'll get used to it."

Canada, I thought, but didn't correct her. I've been living in Canada.

"Girls," I said carefully. "Get off them."

The boys jumped up and ran away. "Not that I'm sure that they didn't deserve it," I said while they were still in earshot.

I looked at Miryam and Jana. "What happened?"

Jana looked at me with her big brown eyes. Her long dark ponytail had almost come out of its elastic.

"The usual stuff, Tamar. They want to bomb our village. Shoot us. You know."

I looked at her. They were the only Arab-Israeli kids in the class. They were cousins.

Miryam grew up in Jerusalem, and Jana lived in Jaljulye. They went to regular Israeli public schools. In the breaks from class they spoke Hebrew to each other.

"I just, I couldn't take it anymore. Someone had to tell them. It was enough already."

I hugged her. "Of course. I said. I understand, believe me. But I don't want you to get into trouble with the school. Just tell me if they say anything like that again. I'll take care of it."

They both hugged me.

I knew what would happen when I spoke to the boys. They'd laugh and their parents would would be defensive and dismissive. The principal would do nothing unless someone seriously got hurt. I took a deep breath and walked into my classroom. I controlled the urge to punch a hole through my paper thin walls.

I taught English as a Second Language beside the bookstore, across from a record store.

For the past few months, I'd been teaching adults but in the summer they run an English summer camp for kids of all ages. I figured it would be less depressing than teaching people who were only a year or two older than me who were studying English to travel or do their Masters degrees in North America or England.

I had no plans. I'd been studying art and photography in Jerusalem but I decided to take a break. It was a competitive program and I wasn't sure what I was going to do afterwards.

My mom thought I should finish my degree and become an art teacher, or come back to Canada and do a different degree. I moved in with my cousins, in the town I grew up in, and got a job at a nearby school. It seemed like a good way to see if I wanted to teach.

Every day I doubted it more.

Some days I kind of liked my job.

The kindergarten kids are my favourite. There's Michal and Yoni, whose mothers are best friends who tell me everyday that they want to marry each other when they grow up. Sometimes they even hold hands under the table. There's Mohammed, the gentle, well mannered little boy whose mother frets everyday is being disrespectful. There's Maya, a little genius who can already read in Hebrew and is eager to learn to read in English. It's rare anywhere, when a kid really wants to learn like that. There's also Shira and her mom, who line up every morning before class to remind me to give her Ritalin in the class break.

Sometimes it's a lot to remember.

I watch a lot of TV and take a lot of photos in my free time.

Sometimes I torture myself by going into the bookstore and flirting with the guy who works behind the cash. His name is Bar. He doesn't talk much, and when he does it tends to be sarcastic. We flirted for a few weeks, and when I finally thought, I can't do this anymore, if he doesn't ask me out soon, I'm going to ask him, he casually mentioned that he has a girlfriend.

Now when he sees me, he looks both happy and guilty so it's less masochistic than it sounds.

I don't even know what I like about him, apart from the fact that he puts aside photography books for me, and he's read just about every book ever written.

I've become friends with the guy who works in the record store. His name is

Yaron and he has blue eyes and long thick eyelashes. He has sandy hair that springs into tightly would curls. I guess I'm not his type, although I have no idea what his type is.

Some kind of hippie? Someone with flowing skirts and glasses? Someone who reads philosophy instead of photography books and short stories.

Sometimes when he smiles at me I think he thinks of me as a little sister.

I guess I should be happy that he's not predatory.

We've started taking our lunch breaks at the same time now. He asked me about Canada and I asked him about travelling in Asia.

"What's Laos like?" I asked one day.

"Like Israel on Yom Kippur, but like, every day."

I raised an eyebrow. "You mean the country just comes to a standstill?"

He smiled. "It's very quiet."

One day he came with me to the pet store across the street to pet the puppies. The guy in the store asked me if he was my boyfriend and I shook my head. He looked confused but I just shrugged.

Today Bar showed up at my work and asked me to go for lunch. We walked through the restaurants below, the Burger Ranch and McDonald's and sweaty Schnitzels that had been sitting on plates for hours.

There were a couple of food stands outside. Let's get *sambusek*, he said and I nodded.

I bit into the hot dough and ran my tongue along my teeth to pick out sesame seeds. It was forty degrees out.

"What happened to your girlfriend?" I asked.

"We broke up like a week ago," he said. "Don't worry about it."

He tried to kiss me at the bottom of the stairs going up to the school. I pulled back. I had no intention of making it that easy.

"You can text me later, I said, I'm done teaching at 4pm." I laughed all the way into my classroom.

By the end of the day, he'd texted me five times.

I felt guilty so I called him.

"Want to see a movie tomorrow night?" he asked.

"Sure."

"I have some good movies at my house, maybe you should come over."

"Okay," I said.

I spent the next morning taking photos of the kids splashing in puddles across the street from the apartment. There was an elementary school whose bells rang to the tune of Santa Claus is Coming to Town.

Yaron came to visit me that afternoon on my break. He sat down in the staff room, and he flipped through the book of photography Bar had given me recently. It was called Drive By Shootings, and it was a series of black and white photos taken by a New York taxi driver.

I smiled. A kid's class was going on outside, and a couple of them were screaming.

"It would be so cool to have my own book like this someday."

He looked at me. "You will." He paused. "What'll it be about?"

I grinned. "Kids, obviously."

"You need a good title."

Outside, another kid screamed.

"I'll get back to you," I said and he smiled.

"Okay. I'm waiting to hear."

I walked back with him to the record store. He made funny mistakes with English speaking customers. "Thank you so much," one of them said. "You're mostly welcome," he answered, and I tried not to laugh.

After work he drove me but he didn't want to come upstairs. My cousins were starting to think there was something going on so I told them about my date with Bar.

He came to pick me up an hour later.

He lived with his parents in an apartment a few streets away.

He kissed me. He had full lips. "Come on", he said and led me to his bedroom.

The blinds were closed and it was full of shelf after shelf of books. A part of me wanted to go through them more than I wanted to talk to him.

He flopped down on the faded blue comforter on top of his bed and pulled me on top of him.

After months of waiting it was weird for things to move so fast.

He pulled my shirt up over my head. "I wanted you since the day you walked into the store," he said, and I laughed. "What? I did."

"It took you long enough," I answered and he laughed.

He was pulling my pants off when his mom walked into the room.

She saw my white underwear and red lace bra before I'd even been introduced.

"Hi," she said, as I scrambled to throw his blanket over my body.

She looked away until I got dressed.

"Bar's mentioned you," she said in English. Would you like to stay for dinner?"

My parents are Canadians who waged an English speaking war in our home, especially at meal times. My brother and I would speak to each other in Hebrew at the table, and our parents would demand we answer them in English or wouldn't get dessert.

Bar's mother is American. His parents separated for a few years after his dad got his secretary pregnant, but they'd been together for five years. His brother was married, and had a five year old daughter. On Friday nights they did family dinners, less out of a religious obligation and more out of convenience.

I nodded slowly. "Okay."

His mom made crispy chicken, roast potatoes and salad.

I spent most of the meal playing with his niece, Amit. Her parents had been trying to have another child for four years, and the tension between them was obvious. I tried not to think about Bar telling me, matter of factly, that his brother saw a prostitute on Allenby in Tel Aviv every two weeks, to "release tension." Bar himself had lost his virginity to a Russian prostitute named Irina when he was in the army. "It was embarrassing to still be a virgin at nineteen," he said. He stopped going after a few months, when he realized he'd fallen in love with her.

I took out my camera and took a few photos of Amit. She giggled, and started posing. I talked to her, to distract her, so instead of making duck faces, I could capture her personality.

I tried to avoid making eye contact with his mother.

Bar reached for my hand under the table.

"So Tamar," his dad, said eventually, "What is it that you do?"

I looked at him. "I work at Wall Street Institute."

His dad looked impressed and looked at Bar.

"She's in finance?"

Bar snorted. "It's the name of a language school. She teaches English, but she's an artist."

I shrugged. "I guess so. I like to take photos."

They looked at me expectantly.

"Sometimes I think about putting together a collection of photos for an art show. There's a gallery in South Tel Aviv that's been interested after I sent them some work. I'm trying to put together some of my latest stuff for them."

Bar looked at me. "What's it about?"

"The show?"

He nodded and they all looked at me.

I looked at his parents. I thought of all the kids and their parents. I thought Liron and Maor, of Miryam and Jana.

"Kids," I said quietly. "I find them fascinating."

His mother smiled at me.

"There's something about them that's so open, whether they're ecstatic or angry or upset, if they're being mean or sweet or annoying, their reactions are always so authentic." I looked away. "I'm thinking of calling it sometimes I like to shoot kids," I continued, and I cracked a small smile.

Everybody was silent.

I heard the clink of the knife as it scraped against Bar's mother's plate. His father stared at me.

Eventually, Bar let out a low and gravelly laugh.

I pulled my hand away from his and got up.

I walked into the hallway and texted Yaron.

Michael Fraser

Michael Fraser has been published in numerous national and international anthologies and journals including: *Paris Atlantic, Arc, CV2*, and *The Caribbean Writer*. He was published in the *Best Canadian Poetry in English 2013*. He won Freefall's 2014 and 2015 Poetry Contests. He won the 2016 CBC Poetry Prize. His latest book is *To Greet Yourself Arriving* (Tightrope Books, 2016).

M
I
C
H
A
E
L

F
R
A
S
E
R

The Black Union Dead

The sun-shattered morning sieves
through bottomlands clapping cadavers
rippled under the tree's tea-green antlers.
Me and Abel crumble low,
hinge and shoulder remains from
the Tennessee's mud-soaked banks.

Their arms fall like downpours
dragged through thickets. They land
with dampened thuds, smudging
the others roped and tagged.
Stink rot is moored everywhere,
from scarred battlefield skirmish lines
to no count bugtowns, bodies gas-bloated,
maggot-gnawed, decayed swill for
scavenging pot-bellied hogs belching
their fill.

When the deceased
mirror our hickory bark shade,
we pause, cripple flickering seconds,
our shovels spearing fathoms of earth.

Walking Home

I thought I had seen everything,
but there I was
under skywaves of dancing clouds
waiting for rain to slobber down

crisp mottled leaves
skittered along the sidewalk
& colored the chalk roadbed
like a line of soft quilt

you said, "autumn"
and I was chained
to your marzipan smile
& snowlight green eyes,
I wanted to touch
the slabs of wind
rolling through your hair

walking beside you,
I felt the oak trees
breathe September right through me.

Grand Junction

I became contraband,
nearabout muled back to bondage
when a copperhead and his consort
let me night in their hayloft,
till I heard him wish General Lee
had triumphed in Antietam and
closed the ball early. I had to
acknowledge the corn before
he grabbed his pig sticker.
I fleet-footed for miles through
torn Tennessee, hitched with fellow
runners ploughing north on holed
wagon roads. We reached Union lines
where pickets led us under spry
moon gleam. We wolfed down
livermush sided with collard baits
before sips of old red-eye laid us
log still. Morning splashed the
Jonah's den we had happened into.
Scores of fellow negroes lay strewn
with heads balanced on haversacks,
some grayback-infected, dew-poisoned
along pipjennies, slumped with shakes on litters.
The strong rooted up for colored regiments.

They were tenderfoot fresh fish
fitted in Northern wool navy sack coats,
cupping lead pill boxes, and shooting irons.
There were top-rail sawbones employing
keen mother-wit in the field hospital.
Near mustered-out Yanks arrived
like fallen timber prone on pushcarts,
others shanks mare. It was butcher's fair.
Sawbones wallpapered the wounded
with pop skull whiskey before severing
limbs clean through joints, the sliced
screams ear-cracking sharp like
chain lightning crisping pealed flesh.

Midlife (after Jennifer Chan)

When will I unearth this living.
Peel its shell and taste the hard light
within. At Sunnyside Beach, the moon's
first toe dips naked in rolling water.
My house is a small ode of bricks, a cog
in a collection of rows. I am a collection of cells.
If I were to choose a name, I'd let it flutter
ahead of me and watch it crumble the front door.
The threshold of wanting. Decades before this
present obsession, I could smell rain and hear
the universe breathing. All those monsters stuck
in closets. I want to name something that isn't there,
find meaning in floorboards, know there isn't mold
lurking behind the drywall. I know existence
would be simpler if I was sound. If I was only a letter.
Unlike matches, I don't begin with fire. I begin.

Stage Four

I remember the first time
her voice feathered up my face,
and how the frisson groundswell
furnished my skin. She was spring's
roric birthstone,
murano glass dressed with light,
the northern spy apple pith minus snow,
even the lake listened and mirrored the
stenciled rust red

                                 stippling her shorts.
Her scent walked with me braided
through July's commodious nights,
and on snapshot days, our cottage hands
freed sand-weathered doors.
            Sometimes,
she wasn't spring's birthstone,
but winter's ice-water falsetto
waving at the solstice.
The judge
arrived as a pulled-tooth hour, and she
felt the slack in her life transpire.
She said the lump sat
growling under
her armpit and my thoughts drained

with the tub. When her fly uptalk coifs
shrank to peach fuzz, we grew with
each shivery shelled word that held us.
The feckless sickroom marathon she
ran failed to offer a crisp prize.
                                    I cite her eyelids,
wood smoke swells blotching beneath,
the chafe and shudder of the
crab's sidewise sty.

J
E
N
I
L
E
E

A
U
S
T
R
I
A

Jennilee Austria

Jennilee Austria is a Filipina-Canadian writer, youth mentor, social service worker, and the founder of Filipino Talks—a program that builds bridges between school staff and Filipino students. Originally from Sarnia, Ontario, she wandered throughout North America and Europe before finally settling in downtown Toronto, where she begrudgingly learned how to kayak.

The Kayaking Lesson

"Welcome to Kayaking with Chris!" the instructor called out. He was a mid-dle-aged man with tanned arms and sun-starved legs. "Came down from Marmora to try teaching some intro classes. If these go well, I can start my kayaking school, so promise you won't make my first TripAdvisor review a bad one!"

We laughed as he handed us our life jackets.

Marilyn was a newly-retired teacher. "I've kayaked once or twice before, but I just needed to stop myself from watching another hour of CP24," she said, eagerly clicking her life jacket into place.

Dan wore sunglasses on the back of his head and shielded his eyes with a sun-burned hand.

"I'm a paralegal by day, but a photographer by passion," he said, holding up a clunky waterproof camera. "The skyline'll be beautiful at sunset, and I'm gonna sell some gems to Nat Geo if I'm lucky." He wiped the foggy lens with his fat finger.

"I'm Lina and I'm new to Toronto," I said. "I read that this class will teach me how to paddle to the Toronto Islands on my own, and that sounds like a great break from the city."

"Hey, you a Filipino?" Chris took off his floppy Tilley hat, his piercing eyes appraising me.

"I was born in Canada—"

"Just got back with a buddy o'mine from the beach area, Bora-Cay," he interrupted. "I loved the Philippines, 'specially the people. I'll tell you all about it!"
"Who wants to be the first one out?" the dock hand asked.
My hand shot up. I clambered into the yellow Tsunami kayak and was pushed out before Chris could teach me how to paddle.

*

After a lifetime on the shores of the St. Clair River in Corunna, Ontario, I'd moved to Toronto two months before university began so that I could slowly adjust to city life. But most nights, I found myself gravitating towards the harbourfront, eating vinegar-doused fries from a white food truck and watching the water, just like I would back home.

I knew only one person in the city: Cindy. Both of our parents had left the Philippines for Corunna so that our fathers could don ill-fitting coveralls, helmets and steel-toed boots to work as journeymen at Imperial Oil, the refinery that was so close to our homes that the smokestacks spewed smelly clouds over our backyards. Cindy was four years older than me, and she had scooped up so many awards in high school that when she chose to study marketing in Toronto, we knew that she would never live in Corunna again.

"You won't believe Toronto, Lina," she'd said to me at every Christmas dinner for the past four years. "It's the opposite of everything you've ever known. Can't wait to show you."

But weeks after I arrived, I discovered that she was secretly dating a Jewish vlogger named Levi and she didn't want to be seen with me.

"I don't hang out with Filipinos anymore," she said during a harried meet-up at Dineen. "It's too hard being lumped in with them."

"What do you mean, 'lumped in'?"

"Levi thinks I'm Chinese," she said. "It's easier that way." She rushed away, latte splashing onto her manicured brown fingers.

*

"Lina! You're gonna hit the dock!"

I plunged my paddle into the water and desperately pulled it towards me, splashing murky lake water all over my lap.

"Paddle on both sides!" Marilyn said, using her kayak to nudge mine towards the open harbour. "Left, right, left, right! And don't stick the whole paddle in—just skim the water!"

I dipped the paddle in gently and pushed behind me. "Left, right, left, right," I said under my breath. And to my surprise, the kayak obeyed and went forward. I closed my eyes, relieved.

"You praying?" Chris asked, paddling past me with broad, confident strokes. "Filipinos are real religious. Met a girl in Bora-Cay who said she'd prayed to meet someone like me. What a compliment, eh? Met her family and I'd never seen so many little brown folks in my life. Felt like a giant. You should've seen the way they treated me, like I was a god or something!"

"Left, right, left, right," I mouthed.

*

Growing up in Corunna, I was never an outsider. I'd had the same classmates since the first day of kindergarten. Even when their pale faces sunburned during a fifteen-minute recess and I looked tanned in mid-January, I was never treated differently. Many of them descended from old Dutch farming families, and they were passionate about only one thing: making the never-ending line of substitute teachers cry.

The substitutes were usually immigrants from Italy and Portugal, and if they couldn't properly pronounce names like Dries, Joep, and Maaike during attendance, the class would dissolve into a shrieking mob of spitballs, airplanes, and even saliva-covered black licorice dropjes aimed at the teacher's hair.
Like all of the girls, I was in love with Thijs, an all-star athlete who was so

worldly that after playing baseball thirty minutes away in Wallaceburg, he came back casually calling it "Wally World" and we all swooned.

One day, he smuggled a snowball filled with jagged ice into the classroom and pitched it straight at the Portuguese substitute teacher, slicing her arm through her white silk shirt. Thijs howled with laughter and got ready to follow up with his sharpest paper airplane yet. As drops of blood pooled onto the teacher's blouse, she looked at me for help.

Before I could think, I stood in front of his desk. "Thijs, that's enough!"

"What's your problem?"

"She's hurt!"

Thijs stood up too, towering over me. "What, so all of a sudden you're brown now? You're gonna stand up for this brown teacher?"

From my point of view, with her chestnut hair and green eyes, the teacher was white. But upon looking at her exposed arm, I realized that her skin was the same shade as mine.

Torn between my love for Thijs and the pained look in the teacher's eyes, I grabbed the airplane and tore it up. "Stop being a dick," I said, scattering the pieces across his desk. "If you're gonna pick on someone, pick on me."

Thijs sat back down.

It should've ended there, but the teacher decided to thank me in the worst way possible.

"Filipinos are such sympathetic people," she said, patting my shoulder. "I knew you would help. You look just like the nurses that took care of my mother."

The entire class screamed with laughter. "Nurse Lina! Paging Nurse Lina! I'm gushing blood and no one else will save me except for a Filipino! Help me, Nurse Lina!"

I slunk to the back of the room, instinctively knowing three things: Thijs would never like me back, I would never become a nurse, and worst of all, without ever leaving Lambton County, I had suddenly become an outsider.

*

My arms ached as I paddled against the waves with clumsy strokes.

"I learned Tay galo while I was in Bora-Cay," said Chris, circling my kayak.

"I don't speak Tagalog."

"May-gan-da ka! May-hal ki-ta! You know what those mean?"

"'You're beautiful' and 'I love you,'" I replied flatly.

He beamed. "And you said you didn't speak it. See, I just taught you something!"

I rested my paddle across the kayak, pretending to stretch my arms. My mom told me that if men ever said things like that to a Filipina, it was because they were trying to marry one.

"You can always tell when they learn languages to get a bride," she would say. "They don't learn how to order chicken and rice, you know."

My mom used to be a waitress at Golden Palace, the only Chinese restaurant in Corunna. With her long black hair, petite frame and pretty face, old men hit on her all of the time. She complained about it until she realized that if she encouraged them, she would get better tips.

She re-enacted everything after each shift.

"And so I said, 'You think I'm pretty? What a sweet man! Come again next week, I'll be waiting for you!'" She'd mimic waving at them with one hand and scooping up the generous tips with the other.

My mom's customer service skills kept the restaurant busy through snow-storms, tornado warnings, and even the intermittent Chemical Valley spills, when the foul stench in the air made us light-headed and the Fox FM announcers warned everyone to stay home with the windows and doors closed.

"Couldn't stay away," the men would say. "No food in the fridge and a long night ahead of me, where else was I s'pposed to be?"

When the chef realized that the customers were coming more for his waitress than his chop suey lunch combos, he replaced my mom with two elderly white ladies who gave a death stare to anyone who dared to ask if the food was authentic.

"Best Beef Boo Boo y'ever had," they'd say. "Youse all gonna order or jus' sit there an' starve?"

My mom never worked again. In every restaurant in Lambton County, she'd have to serve white men, so there was no other option but to stay home.

"Always keep your guard up," she warned me. "Never give them what they really want—or suffer the consequences."

*

Chris led us into Marina Quay West, where the waters were clean enough to see the plants growing below. But around the luxury boats, debris had pooled together at the surface, with beer bottles and take-out containers floating in feathers and dirt.

Japanese tourists in the Music Garden began taking pictures of us. Marilyn waved cheerfully and Dave pulled out his camera.

I smiled and subconsciously tried to position my kayak in front of the floating garbage.

"If you think this is dirty, you should see your own country," Chris called out. "The resort staff even told us we shouldn't bother going to see the coral reefs because they were all dead from being bleached by sunscreen chemicals. The girls kept apologizing for it whenever they saw us. 'Forgive us, sir!' and 'So very sorry, sir!' Gosh, were they ever polite!"

I tasted blood in my mouth.

"We asked them to come tanning with us but they hated the sun. What a waste, living in a country with permanent summer and not wanting to get dark! No wonder their sunscreen killed the corals. But they'd always come out with us at nighttime, y'know what I mean? Filipino girls are really incredible at certain things, you know that, Lina?"

As I desperately tried to turn away from him, my kayak bumped against one of the shiny white yachts.

"Watch it!" a man shouted at me from the deck. "Don't you be denting my boat, this costs more than your life!"

I glared back at him, refusing to apologize.

Chris glided away and spun his kayak around with a showy, sweeping motion that sent the water around him up in a glittering semi-circle.

"I think it's time to teach you all how to turn properly!" he called out.

*

I got a receptionist job at a non-profit in St. James Town, where hundreds of families lived in the cramped apartments above our cluttered office.

Every morning, my supervisor greeted me with a loud, "Lina, you look so professional today!"

I always wore dress shirts, pencil skirts and heels. I knew this was Kristen's way of saying that I was overdressed; everyone else wore faded mom jeans and old knit blouses that had lost their colour and shape years ago. But I was scared that if I let myself dress like them, no one would take me seriously.

"First impressions are more important for us than anyone else," my mom had said while picking out my clothes at Ricki's in Lambton Mall. "You have to control what they think when they see you."

"What do you mean, they?" I asked. "Who's they?"

"You know who," she said, her voice dropping to a whisper. "Canadians."

"I *am* Canadian," I replied through gritted teeth.

She thrust another skirt into my hands.

But the first time I slept through my alarm clock, I threw on an old polo shirt and baggy jeans and tied my unwashed hair into a ponytail. I was about to apologize for my appearance, but Kristen beamed when she saw me.

"Now you look more like our sweet little nannies here in St. James Town," she said, cheerfully giving me more responsibilities than she ever had before.

And as the work piled up on my desk, I spent the day looking at my reflection in the grubby window, wondering why she preferred me like that.

*

"When turning, you have to really lean into it while you make a big sweeping motion with your paddle, just like a big smile. Can you all smile for me?"

We swept the paddles across the water and magically, our kayaks swung towards the skyline as the the clouds broke and a beam of sunlight perfectly lit up the CN Tower.

"What a backdrop!" Dave said, fumbling for his camera. "Best skyline in the world!"

Marilyn smiled at me and I grinned back.

"Now there's the smile from Lina I've been waiting for!" Chris called out. "Dave, get your camera ready. I wanna show you a real trick!" He slid his kayak up against mine, dropped our paddles into the water between us, and stretched his arms across my boat.

"Lina, do you trust me?"

"What are you doing?"

"I want you to stand up!"

"What?"

"Stand up in the kayak!"

"I don't want to!"

"Come on Lina, don't be difficult, everyone's watching!"

I pulled my feet beneath me and sat on the top of my seat. Then, with my arms out wide, I nervously stood up as Chris kept the kayak steady beneath me.

"What a trick, eh? Other instructors would never do this!" Chris called out. "Dave, put this pic up on TripAdvisor, okay?"

Dave snapped a dozen shots just as the sun lit me up in a warm spotlight. In spite of myself, I smiled again.

"Gosh look at her, she's practically pocket-sized!" said Chris. "Lina, you're what, a hundred pounds? Typical Filipino girl-size. I'm telling you, Dave, buddy, there's a country full of 'em and they're so easy—"

Pretending to lose my balance, I stomped onto his kayak and tipped it towards mine. He yelped as a bit of his skin was caught between the boats.

"Yowch! Never had that happen before!"

Without saying a word, I sat down and wiped the smile off of my face.

*

For the last part of the lesson, we ventured towards Billy Bishop Airport.

"If you're using this class to learn how to get to the Islands on your own, here are the rules," said Chris. "Don't go in the area between the white buoys lead-ing to the runway. Don't try to out-paddle a ferry boat coming straight at you. Don't paddle down the middle of the lagoons because kayaks shouldn't hog the deepest part of the water."

As I made mental notes, something large blocked out the setting sun. A huge trumpeter swan with a P24 label on its wing swooped down in front of our kayaks, landing metres away.

Dave giddily pulled out his camera. "This one's for Nat Geo for sure!"

"Can we feed it?" Marilyn asked, rummaging in her pockets.

"No, don't feed him," Chris said, his voice calm and quiet. "He may get sick and he's already endangered."

The swan glided towards me, steadily holding my gaze with his black beak turned straight down.

"He looks pissed," I whispered. "What do I do?"

"He wants you to know that he notices you," Chris replied. "Let him do his thing and treat him with respect."

The swan circled my boat slowly and I held my breath. But when Dave's camera clicked, the swan let out a loud hiss, threw his long neck forward and snapped his beak in my face. I shrieked and slapped my paddle hard against the water, splashing water everywhere.

Still hissing, the startled swan opened its giant wings and swiftly flew back to the Islands.

"You wrecked my money shot!" Dave whined.

"Lina! You were supposed to *respect* him!" Chris snapped.

"But I didn't feel safe!"

"That doesn't mean you should lash out like that. This is his space!"

"But it's also my space," I replied. "Don't I deserve respect, too?"
"I think she does," said Marilyn.

"It was inappropriate," Chris said. "There are rules of conduct and—"

"Oh that's right, I should've just let him attack me," I interrupted, laughing bitterly. "I should've let him bite and scratch me as much as he wanted. And then I should've apologized profusely to him afterwards and treated him like a god, right Chris? I'm glad this lesson is over, because I don't need to learn anything else from you." I turned my kayak with my best sweep stroke yet and paddled back to shore.

*

Back on the dock, Chris congratulated us heartily. "Good news, everyone: you all passed 'Kayaking with Chris' with flying colours!"

Marilyn and Dave clapped politely.

"And since this is my first class, I hope you'll all review me on TripAdvisor tonight. Help a buddy out, okay?"

"I'm not very good with the internet," said Marilyn.

"Sorry, gotta send these pics to Nat Geo while they're still hot," said Dave.

Chris looked at me with hopeful eyes. "If you do this for me, I'll give you a second lesson for free," he said.

"I'd love to," I replied, smiling.

"This is why I always say Filipino girls are the sweetest," Chris said, beaming. "It's like they were born to help people out. Thanks, Lina."

*

The next time I was on the dock, I had a new set of classmates.

There was Isaac from Tunisia, whose life jacket was too small for his broad chest. "Do I really need this if I already know how to swim? You know Oussama Mellouli, champion swimmer of Tunisia? We both grew up on the Mediterranean. I don't need this vest, do I?"

There was Mariela, from Bolivia, who clutched a gold crucifix around her neck. "My mama would never let me do this," she said nervously. "She'd be praying a novena back home if she knew."

A petite, black-haired girl strolled towards us, her voice high and clear. "Who's excited for the lesson to begin?"

Jennilee Austria   273

My hand shot up.

The instructor smiled at me. "Welcome to Kayaking with Kyung," she said.

Ian Keteku

I A N

K E T E K U

Raised by Ghanaian parents, Canadian based poet Ian Keteku is strongly influenced by his African upbringing. His work embraces the Ghanaian principle of Sankofa (returning back to better see the future). In addition, Keteku is a practitioner of Afrofuturism; a philosophy of projecting the black experience into a celestial, technological future.

He travels through eons of time and space, exploring the struggle and joy of being human. He implores the reader to examine the state of their own politics, the nature of their own heart and reimagine a future worth fighting for.

Take Care published in winter issue of I.D.I.O.T. 2017

Moment I

I remember my birth like it was tomorrow
the unholy sensation
of abandon
of accepted struggle.

My mother's womb
a burning revolution
a promise on fire.

I do not recall the choice
to be burning

a broken archeologist
searching for sky
in unchartered ground.

Before my skin,
colour of claustrophobic handcuffs
became fodder and fuel
for a war I was born into.

Clock hands point
towards a verdict
the seat-belt light is off

I crash land into tomorrow.

Fragmented blessing.
Dark-skinned schism.

My cry
so familiar, it is heard in the past
Mother bleeds lament,
we can both see tomorrow.

Point of Boiling

What temperature do memories burn?
Our collective anger sits charred in front of us
taunting it's privilege
amongst the fire.

Ash stains our trembling teeth
our mouths reluctant of water.
Are memories best served warm?

On a silver tongue, dripping river Delta
slave ships and servitude.
In this loud of burning
our faces sing ballads of the blaze.

My roots remember the scars
the smell of Icarus' dream.
And the smoking truth—
fire cannot be quenched
with boiling blood.

And...

And a soft 'yes' serenading mountain top, pensive Appalachian and Himalayan hurt. And an empty Bible and sitting restless and fearful. And once I checked out the story of my life. And returned it, the next day. And I didn't like the author and couldn't relate to the protagonist. And he was too 'not enough.' And I will wait for the sequel. And everything reminds me of autumn—how beautiful must it all be before it all dies again. And I believe in something I am too young to love. And I am afraid, I am too old to know what love is.

Forgiveness

The aged birch
as antiquated as song,
as tall as dreams in the ears of orphans

holds within its belly
of bark and unwavering commitment
a dogma of forgiveness.

For the lumberjack
so hell-bent on bending its branches
slicing it into droplets of tables
and chairs and paper to soak the blood of poets
forgives.

The alloy waters feeding our insecurities
nourish our egos
as we continue to confuse its blue
with items we no longer love,
still forgives.

Allah, give me the mood
of the birch, sun and water.
My apologies run dry
in the damp doorway of pain.

Lend me their souls
so my pardons are true

timeless and luminescent.
That I may one day be broken
and feel brand new.

Winter

Winter is a racist season.

It's callous cold screeches chalkboard
against African pelts.

Forcing us to lather our melanated bodies
with white cream
- to protect us.

The season of white religion,
and crack cocaine.

White Santa with a god complex
blesses gifts upon decent children
too scared of poverty to not believe in him.

Punishing others with charcoal offerings
the colour of us.

Autumn

It is easy to forget
every year we smile at destruction.
Embrace the death of our habitat
like out of work undertakers.

We marvel at the sickening sycamore
write poems about the beauty
of the weeping willow, forlorn
severed dandelion limbs.
But we forget

the changing colours of autumn
from green to yellow
to red to brown to ground
to compost to dust
is death.

Death doth make the leaves change mood

But we smile
because it is pretty
because it is art.

Intermission

my father's fist

and my mother's face

often sang duet

never on pitch

one always louder than the other

i blamed myself

for not being able to compose an intermission

to this symphony of stitches

Elephants

Elephants do not pray for water
do not ask the sky
what it knows of mercy
and expect showers of baptism
in return.

The elephant has faith
somewhere there is water,
will trudge through miles of
suffering and storm just to find it.

I will not ask you to keep
any promise,
most promises are glow sticks
illuminating everything
only once it is broken.

We can pray for mercy
we also must walk towards it
have faith that it is there.

Hope does not reside
in any prime minister, parliament
or president pushing red pills.

It is found by those embossed with embarrassment
dusty and damp
for the first time, again.

The dollar is low
And our worries are high
Still, we walk towards fortune's fountain
until the migration breaks us
—as long as there is beauty in our breathing.

In the next room, a thirsty elephant
drowning itself in faith.

Take Care

take care of the great hunger
a bone basket
parading our inadequate love.

take hold, of all you decided
to break. and unbreak
a brittle bullet, a beautiful sin.

take precaution,
in gavel-like laughter—
the court jester's sabbatical.

he watches horror
calls it professional development
calls it self care. take care

for no map has ever protested
only one way to reach the peak.

no summit fails to honour
the unfortunate parts
which made it whole.

It is always awake

The night is not nocturnal
it hangs still
a warm duvet
smoke in a windless room
hands—hazard sign and hospitable
it is a good night.

We nickname it darkness, branded obsidian
"Only ghosts are alive in the dead
of the night" —we say.

Granted we are scared
and when we are scared
we become everything
but gracious.

We accuse the night for not plagiarizing
the myth we made up about it
night falls into melancholia
knowing it is not the abyss of black
our eyes claim it to be.

The sun, not her first born child
she holds so much more light inside her

she offers constellations as conciliation.

How much swallow must it drink
before it can start breathing again?
The night gets nightmares
every time it thinks of itself.

Rules of gravity do not hold in space
but the weight of our words are holding it down
black, dark, dangerous, mysterious, lightless.

It accepts
this is how it goes
for dark things.

LEESA DEAN

Leesa Dean

Leesa Dean is a graduate of the University of Guelph's MFA program and a creative writing instructor at Selkirk College in the Kootenay region of British Columbia. Her first book, *Waiting for the Cyclone*, was shortlisted for the 2017 Trillium and Relit Awards.

When Saturn Returns

The air smells of rotting apples as I drive up the Slocan Valley, past falling down barns made small by the Valhalla mountains. I'm on my way to Rhoneil's, host of *The Deep Woo* podcast, to record an episode on the Saturn return. As artists, we're both interested in this astrological phenomenon: every 28-30 years, Saturn comes back to its original position in your birth chart and gives you a swift kick if you're not on the right path. The transition is often an exquisite disaster before your life stabilizes, and my experience was no exception— my romantic relationship failed and I watched someone I love die, but from this ugly place beautiful possibilities arose, monsoon-like in their power.

*

Even though I never felt at home in Montreal's East End—I was too English no matter how much French I spoke—I took my time leaving the neighbourhood when I walked out on my fiancé. Alex didn't get any tears, but the Dairy Queen where Quebecois classics were projected outside on summer nights made me cry for some reason. Pyjama pants fanning in the wind, I stopped in front of the Super C where we'd shopped the sales every Saturday. We were perpetually broke for reasons including tuition, booze, debts from too many Mexico trips and Alex's drug problem. The weekly flyer, taped to the closed store's window, advertised half price chicken strips—Alex *loved* chicken strips. I imagined the argument we might have in the aisle, him trying to stock up, me knowing there's no room in the freezer.

Across town, I spent my first night drinking alone in a friend's bed. She was in Australia for a month which gave me my first exposure to being alone, something I'd never really experienced. The alcohol fizzed through my synapses, conjuring images of Alex's confused expression when, out of the blue even to me, I announced my intention to leave him. I may as well have been speaking a different language. Cars revved at green lights on Saint Laurent Boulevard and people in the streets sang their secrets loudly, coated in Jagermeister. In the click of high heels I heard the promise of an ancient hunt—barstool laughter, last call taxies to somewhere else.

The night was punctured by city racket, even with the window closed. No amount of alcohol could bring me closer to sleep. Throughout our kaleidoscope of changing landscapes, the restless rhythms of Alex's breath had always helped me loosen my grip on the waking world. Often, his breath brought me back to places we'd been—an inhale would remind me of the silty brown river at the Mexico-Guatemala border, an exhale would sound just like the wild horses in Olon when early morning air shuddered through their nostrils.

I couldn't sleep without his white noise.

*

For most people, the Saturn return comes as a surprise. Despite recent articles in the Huffington Post and Flare that read more like survival guides, the correlation between our disastrous late twenties and Saturn's version of tough love is not widely recognized. Ambushed, those who don't know find themselves disoriented, strangers in their own lives.

I *knew* Saturn was coming, though. I'd been warned in advance.

Rob was a 28 year old American, learning to read Vedic astrological charts as part of his own Saturn return. He'd left a corporate job in upstate New York to volunteer at a dysfunctional permaculture farm in Chiapas, Mexico, which is where Alex and I found him. There, crops shrivelled and red ants stormed the fruit fields—we spent days hacking at them with rusted machetes. People raved about Rob's abilities, so my second night on the farm, before he knew anything significant about me, I let him read my chart.

We met under a banana tree, each holding a candle because there was no electricity. Condensation from the afternoon's rains glistened and the jungle ticked softly with the night wind. He started with my family history—Mom's disability, Dad's alcoholism, my anxiety. I couldn't believe how much he saw in my chart's intersecting lines. At 25 years old, I had an ambivalent relationship with my job, answering phones in an office. I knew I could do better, but the magnitude of my anxiety, something I was too scared to have diagnosed, anchored me in mediocrity. So when Rob told me I'd eventually have a career as an author and teacher, I laughed. Alex, who was reading nearby, noticed us sitting close. I saw his jealousy, even in the dark.

Rob warned me of my Saturn return: I'd have two years of chaos followed by a clearer sense of, well, everything. But I forgot that part of our conversation. Had I remembered, perhaps I would have navigated those years with more grace. Rob also told me I'd marry a light haired, blue-eyed artist and we'd have a child together. I looked over at dark-haired, French-speaking Alex and thought of the future children we'd already named—Charlotte, Serge and Gertrude. Watching Alex tilt his magazine toward the light, I realized he'd chosen those names, not me.

*

Ten days before I left Alex, I called a helpline in the midst of a panic attack, convinced my fast-beating heart would kill me by dinnertime. I was also in the throes of a psoriasis outbreak—within 48 hours, the usual scabs on my knees and elbows had spread to all parts of my body, including my face. I felt like a lighthouse, warning others away from my ugly, rocky shore.

D, a therapist I was able to see on short notice, asked me typical intake questions. We spent a lot of time on alcohol. At that point, I wasn't yet aware of the connections between anxiety, family history and alcoholism—my chances of becoming an alcoholic were significantly higher than the average person. The previous weekend, I'd had another incident— too much wine at a party turned into me lying in the street at 4 AM, telling Alex I wanted to die. He literally had to drag me home. The next morning, I dabbed Cortisone on my wounds, unsure of where the psoriasis ended and road rash began.

I told D about one of my fights with Alex in front of the Super C, how we snagged on some insignificant detail, maybe about money or a newspaper I'd tossed without asking (he was very particular about his old newspapers). He took a half-eaten pear from the ground and hurled it at my head. It spun through the air like a tiny football until it collided with my cheek.

"What did you do?" D asked.

"I don't know. Nothing. We bought some stuff and went home."

Comforted by ginger tea and D's faux-fur pillows, I told her about a few other physical altercations like the time he spit in my face. When asked why I wanted to continue the relationship, my responses made me realize I'd become one of *those* women, making excuses for abuse. What I didn't yet have the words to explain was this: I secretly admired the complexity of our volatility. After fights, we used the bathtub as our healing grounds, naked and locked into each other while steam filled the bathroom. He was perfect in those moments, as if each minor disaster dug a deeper tunnel to his heart and one day there would be nowhere left to go but love.

*

My friend Lena and I navigated our Saturn returns together as cosmic sisters. After I left Alex, she left her partner after seven years of hiding his crack addiction from everyone, including me. We quit our jobs and used our meagre savings to travel to Morocco where we spent Christmas with a backpack of beer on a dune near the Saharan border. Each time I raised a bottle, a whiff of old leather and camel emanated from my hands. The only noise you could hear was the faint wind of the desert, changing the landscape before your very eyes.

Lena and I created a time capsule, not to be opened for ten years. We wrote letters to ourselves and each other on decorative paper from the Marrakech market—beige, with an image of King Hassan II faded into the background. I don't remember exactly what I predicted for myself that day, but after leaving Alex, I started to feel the pull of British Columbia, my home province. Alex had kept me tethered to Quebec, but now I was free. I was also starting to fancy myself an eccentric writer who drank too much but wrote decent poems. I'd started taking classes in university and my teachers saw something in my lyrical, unstructured stanzas

As time passed and my notebooks thickened, Rob's Vedic predictions for my future started to seem a little less preposterous.

*

During my Saturn return, my mother coached me through the big things, like leaving my job and switching to a Creative Writing degree in university. I also called her every Sunday, see-sawing my way through our conversations, glamorizing the past—camping with Alex in El Salvador where falling mangos woke us each morning, an attempted robbery in Ecuador where we outran the clumsy villains. I told these stories because my mother missed Alex but also because I found comfort in the stability of things that had already happened.

By the second year of my Saturn return, my body had changed. I was still prone to psoriasis outbreaks but they became less intense with a healthier diet and a yoga membership—I was spooked into both by fear-mongering internet articles about single women in their thirties. I had a year to not become one of those people. The erroneous assumption that not having a romantic partner meant I'd be alone forever was constantly in the back of my mind. One day, after realizing I'd lost twenty pounds but still wore the same shapeless clothes from my years with Alex, I crammed them all in garbage bags and dumped them outside my Montreal apartment.

When I was 29, I returned home to Cranbrook for the holidays because I hadn't seen Mom in two years and felt an overwhelming longing for that unmistakable smell of her skin, accentuated by cheap Avon perfume. I hugged her extra long at the airport. The next morning, we sipped brandy-bloated coffees and laughed at jokes from a book she'd bought my father for Christmas—we often read his presents before wrapping them. By our third drink, she told me if she ever left my father, she would move to Kelowna and stay with an old high school friend named "Buffalo Butt" Wendy.

Mom bought me more gifts than usual that year, including an expensive sweater. I saw the price tag at the mall kiosk. We were a thrifty family, but she saw me lingering in front of it, fingering the alpaca wool. I was lost in a memory of Alex and me in Ecuador, buying similar sweaters from a roadside stand in the highlands. The vendor had proudly gestured to a field of llamas behind him even though the sweaters were clearly factory made. Mom also gave me an enormous care package of teas (she must have bought out the whole mall kiosk), a kit to grow herbs on my windowsill, and books written by admirable women, all things that would comfort me during another winter alone.

That night, Mom sipped her way through a bottle of wine while Dad drank all the whiskey—his "cure" for anxiety and depression. Around 2 A.M., with infomercials blaring in the background, my Mom became the nurse again as she guided my father to bed. He looked just like Alex, so tall yet unsteady on his feet, too drunk to put together a sentence.

*

Saturn was still lingering at age 30, but I was getting comfortable in my new orbit. I moved to Toronto for grad school, a city I'd scorned as a Montrealer but soon came to love. My friends were all in the arts, and I didn't have to worry about whether to approach strangers in English or French. I dispatched highlights to my mother via telephone—master classes with famous writers, my feminist roommates, a sudden ability to speak up in class without feeling anxious. My relationship with alcohol was changing, though. I'd started drinking more to cope with the stress of grad school and couldn't seem to navigate the line between getting home safe and blacking out. Sometimes, I woke up and didn't know where I was. In exchange, Mom confided that a bone infection had been ravaging my father's body since Christmas. There was talk of amputation but Mom was hopeful the new IV drugs would work. She asked me not to tell anyone.

In my non-fiction workshop, I started writing about Mom. Only 4'11" with wrists like skinny twigs, she worked as a nurse for twenty years until lifting heavy patients eroded her health. It wasn't just her small size and eventual carpal tunnel, it was the polio. The metal rod in her spine that allowed her to walk upright, mostly. There were bones missing from various parts of her body and she wore pants to hide the scars. I didn't know these things until I was a teenager, only because my grandmother told me in secret. I wanted other people to know what her life had been like.

Mom was about to turn 60, which meant she was entering her second Saturn return. During the first one, she had a miscarriage but later gave birth to me. I wondered what might happen this time—would she finally leave my father and shack up with Buffalo Butt Wendy?

Mom deflected questions about her nine months in a body cast by talking about summers on a farm in Alberta and her mean, alcoholic grandfather. She described how at age 18, she picked up my Dad hitchhiking—not love at first sight but more of an awareness they'd eventually end up together. We began to talk every day, closing the gap between mother and daughter. Eventually, she told me about the body cast. I listened, but didn't end up writing about it—that was her secret to keep. Her birthday was coming in three weeks and finally, she'd be getting a pension cheque. *I'm going travelling!* she exclaimed. I think she meant without my father.

The day of my workshop, I felt like a child at show and tell, holding up my most treasured possession—my mother. People sensed her voice in the essay, and they admired her determination to be a nurse despite her disability. I left the room at break, glowing with familial pride: I came from a strong matriarch and it had been validated by an outside audience. That night, I had a date with a light-haired, blue eyed writer who would become the target of my misguided love based on Rob's chart reading, so I pulled out my phone to see if he'd messaged.

He hadn't, but I'd missed calls from home. Too many.

I thought of my father, the IV, his foot, and thought, *Oh God*.

But it wasn't Dad. It was Mom.

*

Saturn took her with a heart attack. Apparently she had pneumonia but didn't realize it since she was too busy caring for my father. Her lungs, full of fluid, compressed against her crooked spine, eventually cutting off her blood flow. When I arrived in Cranbrook, she was in a coma but with such extensive brain damage we decided to take her off life support. I stayed at the hospital until her last breath, not a peaceful one but a laboured, choking sound that haunted me for years. Afterwards, I joined Dad at the house where we drank hard for weeks until I had to return to Toronto. I was afraid to leave, thought he might die, too. I'd been administering his medication through an IV four times a day and feeding him—he never learned how to cook   but I needed to return to school and try to regain control of my drinking.

Mom's death was the end of my Saturn return. After years of living with anxiety, dreading all the terrible possibilities, the worst had happened and I was OK. From the chasm of her death flowed bright streams of creativity—I'd never written so prolifically than when I was grieving. I imagined Saturn, the god of karma, bestowing me with that gift as a condolence for all he took away.

Within two years, I became the person Rob saw in my astrological chart: after completing my MFA with a manuscript that would go on to be nominated for awards, I started teaching college-level English classes. Teaching was a relief rather than a burden. Like the yoga studio, the classroom was a protected space where anxiety could not reach me. I landed a job teaching Creative Writing in a region carved by fast-running water and mountains, close to where I grew up. I rented the top floor of an old farmhouse in Nelson near the hospital where my mother worked in the seventies. There, I wrote the final stories of *Waiting for the Cyclone* with the windows wide open, imagining the days when my mother walked past my house in her little white uniform.

During my second year of teaching, a fair-haired, blue eyed artist presented himself to me—a new instructor in the Social Services program who'd been given the office next door. He stood in my doorway with a social justice colouring book tucked under his arm and told me about his summer painting murals. Immediately, I felt my mind doing that *thing* again where it assumes anyone who's a fair-haired artist must be the man from my astrology chart— I'd done it so many times it had become a joke. Still, I didn't want to rule out the possibility.

*

At Rhoneil's cabin in the Slocan Valley, we begin recording the Saturn return podcast. The opening music, a spacey punk rock track, keys in and for an hour, we discuss what Saturn did for/to/against us. Rhoneil claims she would never date someone who hasn't already been through their Saturn return because you can't trust people until they're on the other side—they have no idea who they are. I lament how unknown this phenomenon still is and imagine a world where we create community around it rather than fumbling through alone. Both Rhoneil and I share how alcohol became a malevolent force during our Saturn returns and eventually, we had to leave it behind.

What I don't know as we share stories on air is that another major shift is coming. There is a life taking form inside me, a miniscule daughter. She's barely a month old at this point, a joint miracle of mine and the fair-haired artist. Her blood is laced with my family's complex DNA. When the blue plus surfaces on the test, I instinctively call home to tell Mom. Only when my father answers do I remember what I'd somehow forgotten.

Nasra Adem

NASRA is a queer, Muslim, Oromo creator living in Amisk-waciw'skahikan (Edmonton) on Treaty 6 territory. They were the Youth Poet Laureate of Edmonton 2016/17 and are currently the Director of Sister to Sister, an artistic showcase for femmes and women of colour and Black Arts Matter—Alberta's interdisciplinary Black arts festival.

mni wiconi

i walk to the water and feel her building anxiety

i am a trigger

i am her sister

zombied by my own poison

unfamiliar

until I bend at the knees and palm the lands tumbled body

and inhale

the water retreats as i release and i imagine it is a sighing relief

familiar

i have stayed close enough to the bank in fear of forgetting

oh how we forget so strategically

the water then gurgles a faint outline of a name

it is my grandmothers

habiba

Meaning beloved

she who has poured and poured and steady streamed a life

for one man and many sons who knew to drink but not to melt

themselves into their own salvation

habiba, we have not met

unless you count this ocean

unless you count my father's gritting teeth

unless you count the impatient itch i have to find you

and to stretch your name out across the Nile bank

tie it tight to the names our mothers and women lost in the murk of patriarchy

Habiba they say there are 2 times of death

one, of the flesh

two, the last breath that carries your name

i will not speaking your name

Habiba / beloved

the water always remembers

even when we don't

Ethiopia

The first marriage of earth and ocean

ordained by a dream of flesh and spirit

named human

named I in 4 trillion chance

named feminine

named keeper of life

and all of Faith's children

named the deepest mahogany containing

all the world's laughter

wrapped in all the world's grief

What happened here

To the yellow

The sloshing abundance that made us fat

and skin supple with Sun

bellies drooping to kiss the earth in gratitude

remember

the stones we sang into mountains

and the mountains we wittled to beads

that would horizon our chests

remember

the men we let live again and again

and the magic we called by our own name

the way we wove the beams of light tethering us

wrapped them

in red and blue ribbon

kept the chorus of ghosts in time

with our soles

Ethiopia, I will speak your name with all its weight

I will remember, even when they do not.

ˈwo͞oman

where else do lungs search for hope
than within
the arms and hips and honey of familiar laughter
the fearless bodies that have remained flexible for lifetimes
the passing down of remedies for the soft hearted
for the artists
the dreamy, hungry women who bite at the truth's flesh
and stumble drunk on its juice,
into a new more forgiving world
women who were once children who believed in homecomings
Sat, elbows on knees
Palms cradling chin
Waiting to witness the hatching of a new joy
for any tiny miracle that didn't demand a death or hundreds
Waiting, for the mold and lingering glue of old belief
To pull itself a part
A toxic taffy rimming the experience of girlhood
but we will fashion this pain differently then they
finesse this fire back to its origins
as the bringer of life
the initiator of change
we will stay mad and
stay ready

to honour the title of fire keeper

Nasra Adem 311

to flick at the embers with audacious tongues

and stoke our own flame

brilliant as sunrise

fragmented and always becoming

we are here despite the breaking

hopeful in the diligent way you need to be these days

coaxing something beautiful to be born

something that will live and never apologize.

Nasra Adem   313

27

T A N Y A   E V A N S O N

Tanya Evanson is an Antiguan-Canadian writer and performer from Tiohtià:ke/Montreal. Winner of the 2013 Golden Beret Award, she presents spoken word internationally, has released four audio recordings and is director of Banff Centre Spoken Word. She has two poetry collections *Bothism* (2017) and *Nouveau Griot* (2018), and moonlights as a whirling dervish.

Book Of Wings

CHEFCHAOUEN

This mountain hides itself in cloud and homes are whitewashed lunar blue. The language barrier is a rich, obstacled Berber. I live in the medina, please leave me alone.

"The time for women in the hamam is now," says the old man shoveling perfumed wood into the oven as I walk past. His back is arched from repetition, stooped over embers glowing in early sun. There is a cold which touches bone this morning. It is a privilege to recognize when one can move from sea to sun to silence. The curved tree, the hanging mirror on a blue city wall, slippery cobblestones lend themselves well to a fallen glance from an indigo man in a snow white jellaba.

Bismillah, the call to prayer came early this morning in Chefchaouen. The tourists are still drunk in their stupor after having been awakened by it at 3am. Loudspeakers emanate from the mosque minaret off Plaza Uta El-Hamman. The call is not for infidels or unbelievers, but I cannot be certain, I am still sleeping.

"This is the land of God!" says Mohammed, refilling my teacup from most high. I am breaking the fast to prepare for the day's walk up the Rif massif.

Women! Limit not your movements! Lift your robes and run into the mountains!

Shriek in response to Barbary apes and Allah! Or come sit with me and sip mint tea under a shy, textiled overhang. There is enough space in this cloud for all, I see it. I find music for all senses, all humours. Blood, phlegm, choler and melancholy escape unwarranted. Be silent, I say to myself. Observe and allow yourself to be observed by leaving the common skin to itself. Be modest. Look, don't touch. Let my troubles invite you into life as a poetic event with each tiny movement fundamental to the next. There is a secret knowledge inside the body framework. The corporeal disappears. Throw this essential scent of joy and death to all on the Path. Float on the gathered pebbles, feel the Mediterranean beneath you undulating in the pavement, or perhaps they've put opium in our tea.

REFUGE

Sidiq was a small effeminate man with narrow frame and loose black curls atop the head. Honey-skinned, a drop of African ink in him still. At 36, he proved intelligent but obstacled by a firm belief in God as an entity outside himself. This transient fervour was both a discredit and a downfall.

Feral dogs moved into attack position as we walked together among the cedars of Gouraud Forest north of Azrou, a small town at the crossroads of Middle and High Atlas.

Two beasts leapt out from between thick trees. Silent first, then suddenly barking as they raced towards us. We bent to pick up stones in our defense, pretended to throw them and the dogs receded.

Sidiq and I walked for hours in hot sun on stone paths between carpets of blood opium poppies. Conversation came easy, but when we sat, the suitor revealed himself. I gently declined the advances, but he persisted. Eventually, I changed the way of my legs to suit the rain.

Leave all other notions behind you, my friend. They are best kept buried in the communal place of unknowing. How many times can the word "no" be negated? The only offer I accepted was to meet his friend in the medina next day, a young Montreal poet named Louis.

Introductions and talk into early morning, the wine took all memory of the night except for feelings of fullness and the poet's gaze. I was charmed into staying over. Louis offered both Sidiq and I a separate bed in the empty, two-story house that he had been renting for the past two months. I prostrated myself into dream.

In the dream I had a meeting with a man. I could not see his face. He was waiting for me at the wrong place, standing beneath ancient ruins. Was it Alexandria or Pergamum? It begins to rain. Unknown insects fall to the ground. Snow falls in with the insects. I find the temple I am looking for and it begins to rain scarabs. I pick one up from the snowy ground and remove its carapace, licked its inner meat. I ask my friend what this means. He tells me it is a wet dream. A dream of things coming to an end. "I know better," I say. Even when you sense apocalypse, pluck some of it off the ground and feast. The next day, Louis invites me to live with him. Boots afoot and shawl to the wind, I leave early morning, whore-like, gliding down the alley where storekeepers rub sleep out of their eyes and take note of my passing.

THE REPUBLIC

Je vous présente mon déclin. De toute façon et de façon facile, un échange s'introduit pour m'apporter un destin tangible dans la journée brillante. Je suis une sorcière mais ce n'est que par accident, je vous le jure.

At times you arrive only to leave without leaving an impression, at others, you change direction quickly, and instead of heading into morning, you answer an invitation from the friend. At that moment, robed men offered me cigarettes from the balcony of their rented hotel rooms and so I moved in with Louis immediately. Dommage, mais beau dommage *que je suis là à vouloir la solitude que seul un autre écrivain peut m'offrir. Peut-être que j'ai le charme dans les cheveux.*

Somewhere in immediate love with this new human, I find the importance of well-brewed gunpowder green tea, sugar shaved from a giant white phallus and mint leaves jutting out the top of teapot. Man and mint, tea and hunger, the length of time in preparation equal to one-third saliva production. Ah, this elegant anticipation, nothing is as sacred or as profound as this service. I just want to be alone with You, a return customer scared of her own reflection. You make me slightly weak in the knees. I am transformed at higher speed than normal. O to pick my nose in the possible Presence! I arrived in parts but managed to put myself together with bread and clothing, good hashish, possible sex and Louis in la République d'Azrou. A little solitude before the fire please, let us pray neither of us runs out of oxygen from the flame. I am not ready to finish my breath practices just yet.

DEAD

After five inseparable nights, Louis and I part. The break preceded by a night of extreme drunkenness among Muslim men whose wives forbid them drinking at home. They come to us instead.

I had left the party early, leaving the men to their red wine and soccer gossip as the night descended above the glass-covered courtyard living room. I awoke dreamless early next day beside Louis in deep REM. I rose to use the bath-room, and in the living room a face offered no reflection. The brown-skinned, thick-moustached man—an unnamed part of the night's festivities—lay on his back, immobile, eyes towards the bright sun above, no movement, a chest of lid, mouth open wide with thick red vomit caked out the right side.
He had died there after the kind of night where good men refuse food to intoxi-cate themselves further into violent confusion. The glass of red had been put up to the test of ensuing nausea and death. I had left the party early to write. Once in the next room, I had nothing to put down. I drank water like vodka, afraid of my own sex, swollen in His direction. Perhaps I am here for you to come and collect me. Walk, walk, my Love. Your very step gives me sign of sub-mission. In the end, the man was not dead at all, only dead drunk. He eventual-ly stumbled home to a wife's possible wrath.

Vérité. Tout change. On se prépare. On n'est jamais prêt. Ce matin, je m'étais
réveillée avec la mort sur les lèvres. Ces voyages me font peur. Aide-moi,
Rimbaud, mon amour."Je suis sûr que je suis plus intéressant que Rimbaud,"
me déclare Louis. La folie me touche. Je la repousse. C'est le jeu de l'univers.

ESCAPISM

After one night apart, Louis knocks on my hotel door and suggests that we
leave town and travel to Fez. Judging by the importance of drink and cigarette
when I am the only woman in a Moroccan hotel bar with a boy who needs to be
saved from himself, what good can come of this?

He is no good to me in bed, but good. I can see that I will eventually abandon
him like I had been abandoned two months before in Paris. It was as though I
had relived the end of my previous relationship only to have the roles reversed.
Why, in the land of God, did you leave me?

Louis is immense. If I stay here I will be destroyed along with him. Our dis-
cussions edge the fantastic but it is a long and guarded border: the weight of
water, the spirit located, the death of God, the Six Bardos. Two writers should
not take up residence and expect to get anything but work done, the work and
the living become wholly inseparable. There is such an equal exchange that
the writing can barely capture the moment before another arises with such
intensity!

I'm tired of wearing long skirts in the street. First lesson in sun: always cover yourself in the heat of day. In the West, we do the opposite. We only think we burn. Here, there is a different burning beneath layers of Muslim cloth.

Louis kisses me impulsively on the mouth as we walk down a crowded Fez colonial street. Louis feels a finger poking his shoulder and we hear the words, "La, la, la!" No,no, no! The conservative fool takes young boys at night. Holds grown men's hands by day in Muslim streets. There is no public affection between the sexes here, it is haram, we have been reminded. I am in the Fez Ville Nouvelle of wide roads and constant cell phones. They tell me the medina dates back to medieval times. Moroccan time exists outside itself, no space, no causality. Do not be afraid of solitude, simply use your cell phone to prove public friendships, especially when sitting unemployed in cafés or standing in long line ups waiting for meat or museums. Life with humans wears a public exterior.

A black cat has come and gone. Is it a sign? The sign was my acceptance of your touch. But this new man lives only in his mind. His body long lost to acts of human stress repetition, devoured by its own schizophrenic tenant. Our conversations could be short, lightning or end up lengthy and painful with the corporeal ravaged like the face of Burroughs or Bukowski with their joint 100 years of work under the virility belt. Veins on the nose, a spotty face in cheeks sunken like boats attempting a River Styx crossing—unsuccessful because they still live. Wrinkles, the only waves left. Bony ass, arthritic hands unpleasant in the end, but what Poetry! An explosive knowledge rendered Absolute. A molecule of Allah in all the pages. All this alongside dark pink vomit the result of bad Moroccan wine and the shit of the Depressed.

STRONG WILL TO MAKE FLAMES APPEAR

We do not hear the call to prayer in this loud modern mess that is Fez. The Truth becomes unforgettable in all the remembering. This is my prayer. It passes through the fingers, engulfs the head, WATCH OUT! Vices are everywhere. Prayer is good breath into actual air, into ominous skies full of storks flying low and formless. We wait for the storm. Gray is not a shade which compliments.

I'm an old fart at 30—flawed, scarred and sagging. Mirrors complement me on my use of gravity. I'm still trying to relate to the aging process as it manifests itself slowly like a vine. Before long, we are covered. This muscle pulled easily, that silver pubic hair, suddenly a strange symptom occurs: a burning, though not for human delights but for all that is, for the secret inside all the events of the world.

Hooded like a black child or a prophet, my young lover slips past our hotel doors and into the city for cigarettes and beer. We take our poison lightly, persistently, and in private. Never forget the value of intoxication. I couldn't see his voice, you see, his voice made love to me. It hit me fully with the Voice of Voices, the giant embrace.

I pray in all directions while he is out. If the sun were shining I could at least know Mecca on this main street. Perhaps putting one foot in front of the other is a way to begin. Louis takes a step towards tangibles. I take one in the other direction. But we are linked by the remaining leg.

"How do you pray? In all directions?" asks the man holding the teapot. He places it on the table and demonstrates the movements, "Berbers place fingertips on the temples with elbows raised straight ahead. How do you pray?" he asks again, now pouring the potion from most high. I say, "It's personal."

These days you need strong will just to make flames appear. If I stay I will die a slow death with this young lover too drunk to look up from his scribblings. The writer in shawls has to sit or move to keep the pants from falling down. Vegetarianism is not always appropriate abroad. This new man is not the end result but a part of the organic process. I take refuge in him because in my state, there are still too many people around, even from my lavish windowsill.

Ah, but to have such a lover, both our mouths dry with experience and western pharmaceuticals threatening to calm our breakouts. Together, we make one Janus—one body, one head, two faces. He takes pills to calm the hallucinations. What does your lover take? Do not let it scare you. Let it be a welcome guest, like a gift from God.

LIGHT

Ma vue s'éclaircit lentement. Le ciel est privé de nuages. Je plane. Je vis mon avenir à chaque instant. Je lutte et j'ai les culottes trempées. Je ne peux pas nier ce que m'apporte l'amour naturel. Lumière. Un couloir vidé se remplit— non—ce qui existe déjà se manifeste devant mes yeux. Mes yeux s'ouvrent à la puissance d'action. Comme dans les tempêtes de sable, il faut se momifier pour passer à travers. Il faut être plus feu qu'elle.

We take a grand taxi back to Azrou, transitional smooth. The Light does eventually come. My legs fold easily now. The only natural position is lotus or half. Trance comes at odd times. The key to a solid meditation is not moving, though I moved to tell you this. Louis goes out for coffee in the morning, he does this to remember civilian life in the village. I pray all the time, the zikrullah of no end, his kiss joins my prayer before stepping out into the medina. His leaving, I do not mind, but for him to have forgotten his dreams, that, I cannot forgive. I rush to clean, pray with incense, eat and smoke hash so quickly that I nearly burn my lip. The fire is ready. I accept that I need help. I light fire out of my hair, the brilliance! I need not move to have union with God or be awake to God. Stillness is key. Stop for a *second damn it*. *"Il ne faut pas chercher à être poète, il faut l'être, ou ne pas l'être," dit Hassan.*

Just then Louis returns from the café in time to catch me off guard. I wipe the sweat from my brow knowing my body is scarred beyond recognition. All is well. I have voluntarily moved into the shade. Consumption itself needs a purge. A purge is always a good idea. I see now, there is beauty, even in death, even in my inabilities, in my failures, there is light.

Ashley Hynd

Ashley Hynd lives on the Haldimand Tract and respects the Manidoosh, Niiwozid, Bineshiinh, Gaa-babaamaadagewaad, Attawandron, Anishnawbe, and Haudenosaunee relationships with the land. Her writing often grapples with the erasure of her history, both as an act of reclamation and a call of accountability for what has been lost.

She was longlisted for The CBC Poetry Prize (2018), shortlisted for ARC Poem of the Year (2018), and won the Pacific Spirit Poetry Prize (2017). Her poetry has appeared in *ARC poetry*, *Canthius*, *Room*, *PRISM International*, *SubTerrain* & *Grain*.

Her hobbies Include trampling the patriarchy, avoiding doing the dishes and getting lost in conversations.

28

A
S
H
L
E
Y

H
Y
N
D

a spoonful of sugar
(helps the medicine go down)

the only proof that I am native is a story
my mother can half remember told
by my great grandmother about how
Sitting Bull and Tecumseh where both
there the day that Custard died
guess that's the problem when you add
cream to your coffee—it gets too white—
stops being coffee starts being cream

My partner reads Gregory Scofield

he pulls his teeth through the pages
clean of the blood spilt by the words
sorrow slack in the corners of his mouth—
eyes are liars—I think we all knew that
when we first looked settlers there
still we gave them everything the tea
                              the furs
                              the land
fools in the folly of self like other
no words for small-pox blankets
                        or rapacity

                        only ceremony
so we gave them everything and they
pull their teeth through the pages
clean of the blood spilt by the words
and I am with him   like treachery
                           like treason
                           like treaty
two rows of purple against white
each on their own path   wondering
                        how the river
                        got so wide
                        was it the tea

                    fur
                        land giving
                              -way

post-colonial relations
(for the missing)

You make arrow heads
of our tears—tell us we are
a reoccurring nothing

leave us empty as ashes
blown by the wind

say you love us
only you never
use the words

just hands
and fingers
and faces

sometimes
it gets so confusing
we want to scream
Armageddon

to see if you blink
but resistance is futile
you are inhuman

your eyes where made
for one purpose
one purpose only

to rob us of our skin

peel back our layers
expose us

to make arrow heads
of our tears

tell me I am
a reoccurring
nothing

Post-colonial Sea Salt [1]

La Baline sea salt
from the clear blue
Mediterranean

sea is evaporated
to a sparkling

                    White

by the sun and sea
breezes.

Connoisseurs
of groumet foods   talk
of sea salt as being

                    essential

                    to north America

eating.

[1] *Found poem made from the writing on the back of a jar of sea salt*

On being published for the 1st, 2nd, 3rd time

If I can write the poems
so that they get published
in a white man's world

then maybe

I can finally feel
like I belong
in my skin

Reconciliation

Quantification:

I can only access my culture through Manitobah mukluks and Ted Andrews' Spirit Animal Guide heritage stripped away by my grandmother's husband left wondering was it who she loved or preservation called performance because my spirit aches for what it has always known was missing still we betray our blood memory every time the knowledge in my body doesn't line up with the words passed down residential school survival our cultures have always learned from each-other or has sun dance already been lost to us

Colonization:

we do it for them
in the status quo threads
of blanketed identity

Abyss

Between the nestled mouth

of the crown and the sullen

burial of history   lays the golden tongues

of our fore-fathers—forked

road that leads to the cemetery

where raven laid flame to rest

where Zeus became   swan lain with woman

and still somehow was more

acceptable—jichaag

galvanized for the taking

Captain Injun

"I know you bought that one" he says, smirk sideways
                                            (of course I did!)
a long unsettling hesitation stirring dust round its feathers
                                            (how else would I have gotten it?)
half-breed essence escaping my pores,   (he's onto me)
"there's nothing wrong with supporting
our culture" I say, "we have a right

to make a living too" (Maybe he'll see right through it   maybe he'll think
'she's holding a pinch of salt calling it sugar'   maybe he'll agree
and that will be our tell, the way we know
that we both know each-other
in some form of memory trapped
in deluded diluted blood

"hmmm" he says, his fingers running dove tailed wing
                                            gently
                                                so gently,
a ghost of a touch whispering secrets I can't translate
 "I suppose we must move with the times"   (I've got him now,
                                                    no escaping!)
"still I think we've lost our way in all this"

handing me the wing—deer antler smooth beneath finger
—feathers pressing outwards from sinew noose round neck
ghost touch lingering in the dust   "maybe it was never ours"   I say,

the taste of gift tumbling round in my fingers

P
R
A
T
A
P

R
E
D
D
Y

Pratap Reddy

(published in *Maple Tree Literary Supplement* in 2018)

Pratap Reddy moved to Canada in 2012. An underwriter by day and a writer by night, he writes fiction about the agonies and the angst (on occasion the ecstasies) of new immigrants from India. He is an alumnus of the Humber School for Writers. He has received the 'Best Emerging Literary Artist Award' from the Mississauga Arts Council. His work has been selected by 'Diaspora Dialogues' for their mentorship programs. He is the author of two published books: *Weather Permitting & Other Stories* (Guernica Editions, 2016) and *Ramya's Treasure* (Guernica Editions, 2018). His new book *Remaindered People & Other Stories* is yet to be published. He lives in Mississauga with his wife and son.

The Lime Tree

It was only a coarse brown envelope from home but it fetched a smile of
pleasure in me. I had been feeling low, facing an uncertain future as an
international student studying in Toronto. I had been planning to write to my
father for advice and assistance but had thought better of it.

I knew what the package would contain—a copy of my sister's first book of
poetry. She was in her early twenties like me, but was already being noticed as
an animal activist and a writer. I was flipping through the slim volume when a
poem's title made me stop. I started to read:

A tree so beautiful
Like nothing on this earth
It could've only been transplanted
From some celestial arbour

Even as I was reading, memories jostled their way into my mind...

You can see the tree when you round the last corner on the way to Grandma's
house. The tree grows in her neighbour's lot. But we aren't looking: I'm busy
with a game on my phone; my sister Mithuna has her head turned away, gazing
at the hillside to our right; Auntie's in the middle of her customary joust with
the taxi-driver about the steep fare from the railway station.

Auntie is Daddy's second or third cousin. For the last two years, she's been chaperoning us on holidays when our parents are tied up with their fledgling consultancy business.

The taxi comes to a stop in front of Grandma's house. The driver toots pom, pom, pom-pom-pom! As we step out, Auntie emits a loud gasp. Thinking Auntie's being strangled by the irate driver I turn my head with interest, but Auntie's staring in the direction of our neighbour's compound. Then I too notice the object which has triggered her amazement.

Resplendent in a garment verdant
Bedeck'd with fruit that shine
In the clear morning light—
Like jewels rarely seen

It's the same lime tree which looked so emaciated last year that Mithuna joked that it was suffering from scurvy.

Grandma comes to the front door, beaming. Close on her heels is the new maidservant Nirmala, also beaming. Presumably catching the contagion from my grandma—though she has never seen us before. Grandma hugs Mithuna and me, enveloping us with the smells of old age and the day's cooking. I'm surprised to notice how much she seems to have shrunk. I remember her as a strong, tall woman. But then again, I've put on nearly a foot since we last saw her.

"Smile, child," she says to my sister. Mithuna had been difficult throughout the journey—sometimes overexcited, sometimes morose, but always managing to annoy Auntie. And Grandma says to me: "How tall you've grown!"

I avoid my sister's eye. We're twins, I'm older by a few minutes, but we look so different from each other that nobody would take us for siblings even. We're fifteen years of age. I'm fair of skin, tall and strong for my age. On my cheeks, there's already a shadowy presence of facial hair. I love sports, and play soccer and tennis. I'm good at studies too, especially math.

My sister's small build, almost scrawny, and looks more of a child than a teen-ager. She's coffee-bean brown, taking after my father. In a colour-conscious country like India, her dark complexion is deplored by aunts and grand-aunts who see a dim future for her in the marriage market. While my twin's no great shakes when it comes to schoolwork, she reads a lot and occasionally writes poetry.

Grandma's house is not large—it has three or four rooms. Apart from a kitchen and a bathroom; it's surrounded by tall, leafy trees, and the old tiled roof is apt to leak when it rains hard. It's dark inside, memories and secrets lurk in its nooks and corners.

I'm the first to go to the bathroom, a small box of a room with cement floor, and only one tap. For hot water, you've got to dip into a large urn which is heated by burning firewood in an opening on the outer wall.

After all of us have bathed, we sit down cross-legged on mats in the kitchen for lunch. It's uncomfortable, but how delicious the simple meal tastes —piping hot—made from fresh ground spices, and vegetables picked the same morning from the back garden.

"Unless you eat, how will you grow tall?" says my grandmother to Mithuna who had refused a second helping.

"Mithuna's always picky about food. In fact, she's fussy about everything!" snorts Auntie.

"Leave her alone, Auntie" I say. "You know she's still quite upset."

"Are you thinking about what happened last year, love?" says Grandma to Mithuna. "You must learn to let go dear."

Mithuna purses her lips. There's an awkward pause for few moments.

"The pickle is so fresh and delicious!" announces Auntie, prompting Grandma to give her another dollop of the pickle made of wedges of sunshine-yellow limes, green chillies, and slices of ginger soaked in brine.

"I made it last week with the limes Kumuda gave me," says Grandma.

Kumuda is our neighbour in whose front garden the lime tree grows. She's a cantankerous woman who has no patience with children. She's always rude to us and wears a permanent frown on her face. It comes from not having her own children, the servants say. I don't remember a time when our neighbour didn't complain of the noise we made whenever we played in our compound. We referred to her as Komodo Dragon—a name coined by Mithuna—rather than as Kumuda-Auntie as well-brought up children ought to.

"Kumuda's lime tree has started giving fruit all of sudden, it seems," says Auntie. "It looked so hopeless last year."

"From what I heard she followed the advice of some tantrik, and within months the tree started flowering," says Grandma.

"Tantrik!" I exclaim. "Does anyone seek a black-magic guy's advice in this age!"

"I wish the tantrik had given her advice on how to have children," says Auntie. "The servants used to joke that her lime tree was as barren as Kumuda."

"If I were you, I wouldn't gossip with servants," says Grandma. Mithuna and I look at each other and smile.

Standing foursquare to the elements:
Shrinking from summer's hot embrace
Rejoicing in monsoon's wet kisses
Shrugging off winter's cold shoulder

The afternoon is warm and sultry. The breeze from the distant sea has not yet begun to infiltrate through the coconut groves along the shore. Under the creaking fans, we stretch ourselves on straw mats. Auntie, in addition, uses a small hand-fan made of coconut fronds.

At four o'clock in the evening, I'm awakened by the bustling in the kitchen. Grandma's making evening tea. Auntie gets up reluctantly; she needs to make a show of helping Grandma.

"Where's Mithuna?" she asks, seeing the unoccupied straw mat. "Mithuna! Mithuna!"

I sigh as I also get up, and say: "She must have gone up the hill, I'm sure."

"That girl! What's wrong with her!" says Grandma, coming into the room.

"Only you can guess," says Auntie to me, "what your twin-sister's up to."

I go outside, and make my way to the back of the compound. Scaling the low wall, I scrabble up the hillside. I spot Mithuna. She's scouring the hillside with her palm over her brow to shield her eyes from the afternoon sun.

"Mithuna! Do you still hope to find Whimsy after all these months? Be reasonable," I say.

"There's nothing wrong in hoping," says Mithuna.

On the last day of our holiday last year, Mithuna's pet dog—a small, furry Lhasa Apso—went missing. We had spent the entire day swarming up and down the hill, shouting for Whimsy until our throats were hoarse. A weeping Mithuna had to be forcibly bundled into the taxi which was taking us to the railway station.

"How can you expect a small pet dog to survive for a year in the wild? Come, let's go back. Grandma is making tea and tiffin for us."

A tired and sweaty Mithuna follows me halfheartedly as I walk away.

"When Daddy said he'd get you another puppy, you should have taken up the offer," I say.

"Like buying a new pen to because you misplaced the old one?"

"Sorry girl. I know, it's not quite as simple as that."

I too had liked Whimsy. He was our parents' gift for Mithuna on our thirteenth birthday. (I had received an adult-size bicycle.) I remember the first day the pup came home. You'd have taken him for small ball of wool but for the eyes which sparkled when they caught the sunlight from the windows.

When we return to the house, Auntie says with a trace of scorn in her voice: "Did you find your Whisky on the hill?"

"Do I look like a drunkard to you, Auntie," says Mithuna, in her rare attempts at conversation with elders.

"The name's Whimsy," I say peaceably, "just for the record." At the time when

Mithuna christened her pet dog, she was madly into Dorothy Sayers. She's still crazy about mystery novels.

Ignoring us, Auntie fans herself, waiting for the tea and bajjies Grandma's making.

In the entire universe,
Like you there's none
A creation of some fabulist's pen:

An ugly duckling of a shrub
In a twinkling, turns into
a swan of a tree
What elixir, what penance or blood sacrifice
Has wrought this magical makeover?

The next morning after a breakfast of dosas and chutney we lounge in the verandah, sipping coffee from steel tumblers. The sky's downcast, as if on the verge of tears. A cool breeze blows down from the hills, ruffling the treetops.

There's no TV or computer in the house to keep us occupied. For want of anything better to do, Mithuna and I set out to explore the overgrown lot around the house, hoping to spot a snake or stumble upon an ant-hill.

"Don't go too close to the old well!" Auntie shouts after us, diligent as ever, referring to the disused well with its windlass falling to pieces in the back yard.

We find a pyramid of logs stacked against a back wall. Stuck into a log is an axe. Plucking it out, I start chopping wood just for the heck of it.

After a few minutes, Mithuna says, "May I try, please?"

Glad that Mithuna's at last showing interest in something, I hand her the axe. "Be careful," I say.

Soon we tire of the sport and go back into the house. Mithuna finds herself a detective novel in our late grandfather's old collection, reeking of must and bygone years. Not finding any writers of my choice, I settle for PG Wodehouse, Daddy's favourite author.

Dear tree, once you too had been
unwanted, unloved, and barren
But now-

The pride of your mistress's life,
Her triumph, her treasure.
So bountiful, so fecund,
Inviting the evil eye of passersby

We spend the evening pottering about in the unkempt front garden. Auntie's examining the wild shrubs as if she's a botanist. Nirmala's plucking flowers for the evening pooja.

"How lovely Kumuda's lime tree looks!" Auntie says, gazing up at the tree.

"Doesn't it? Kumudamma is so proud of it," says Nirmala.

"What fascinates me is that it had looked so...so undernourished last year. But look at it now—it's laden with fruit!"

"The tantrik's cure did the trick I suppose."

"What did he recommend?" asks Auntie, all ears.

"You won't believe this...He told her to bury a dead animal under the tree."

"What! But where in the world did Kumuda find a dead animal?" asks Auntie.

"Well, Kumudamma asked Venkatesh, her servant-boy to help her. As he couldn't find one readily, he killed a small dog he found roaming on the hillside, I believe."

I curse inwardly as I hear Auntie say: "Dear me, what kind of a dog was it?"

"A small fluffy dog, I was told."

Nirmala goes into the house with her flower-basket overflowing with jasmines, completely oblivious to the stink she has left behind. Mithuna starts wailing: "My dog! My poor dog! That horrible woman had my Whimsy murdered."

Mithuna begins to run, heading for Komodo Dragon's house. I hurry after her and physically restrain her.

"Lemme go! Lemme go!" Mithuna's screaming all the while. I've a hard time trying to control her.

"Mithuna, why are you shouting?" asks Grandma, suddenly appearing in the veranda as though the commotion has flushed her out of the house.

"Nirmala said that Komodo Dragon got my Whimsy killed!"

"What nonsense!"

"A tantrik told her to bury a dead animal under the lime tree. I want to know if it was my Whimsy."

"But it's late in the evening now," says Grandma. Komodo Dragon's front door is shut, battened down for the night. "I'll talk to her in the morning if you like."

"Your grandmother's right," says Auntie. "Let's not do anything rash."

"Let Grandma handle it," I tell Mithuna. "We are just visitors here. Grandma has to live with her neighbours every day."

Dinnertime is sombre and silent, and grandmother wisely doesn't serve Komodo Dragon's lime pickle despite Auntie eyeing the jar which stands in a niche. Mithuna eats poorly as usual, but nobody has the heart—or the energy—to nag her. She's quiet, but it's not the quietude that comes from resignation, it's as if she's waiting, treading water until the epic confrontation with Komodo Dragon.

When Mithuna has left the room, Auntie says as she's clearing the dinner things: "It was such a barbaric act. How could Kumuda do it?"

"Being a city-dweller," says Grandma with a pinch of contempt in her voice, "you may not be familiar with the ways of people in small towns. Burying a carcass under a tree is not so uncommon. It's supposed to act as a natural fertilizer. That it was our pet dog is another matter."

The night is restive—like the proverbial lull before a storm—and we go to bed early. But around midnight I wake up with a start, not knowing what had roused me. Moonlight filters in obliquely, showing some furniture, hiding others. Then I hear them, the spasmodic thwacks of a woodcutter. Who would want to chop kindling for the bathroom urn so late in the night?

Then I realize that the sounds are not coming from the back of the house. I rush to the front door —it's unlocked, rattling against the jamb in the wind. When I go out, I see Mithuna's silhouette in the eerie moonlight. She's determinedly hacking at our neighbour's lime tree.

A miscreant intent on violence
has unleashed such havoc,

that in one fell swoop
has reduced a legend to dust

Before I could call out to Mithuna, the scene is ablaze with light—the verandah lamp of Komodo Dragon's house has burst into life. The front door opens, and Komodo Dragon dashes out shrieking, "What are you doing?! What are you doing?!"

"Doing the same thing you did to my Whimsy. What harm had that sweet little dog done to you?"

"What are you talking about? I know nothing about your dog. You've killed my tree. I had nursed it back to health as if it were my child. Now I have nothing... nothing."

"The dog you buried under the tree was like a child to me," says Mithuna.

"I had nothing to do with it. I had entrusted Venkatesh to do the job. I don't even know what he put under the tree."

Komodo Dragon bursts into tears. The ground's littered with fruit, and the tree's doubled down, as if bowing its head in shame.

"Why did you have to do such a thing?" I say, leading Mithuna back to the house. "Grandma would have spoken to her."

"Would that have brought my Whimsy back? Would they have thrown Komodo Dragon into a prison?"

"If I were you, I'd have let grown-ups handle it."

"You're not me, my dearest twin. I've realized long ago that you can't rely on others to fight your battles. You'll have to do it yourself."

Grieve not, lime tree
The scythe of the Reaper
Awaits us all
Death's not the end,
Just a momentary hiatus:
The seed from your fruit will flower yet again.

The next morning I wake up with a feeling of dread. But by that time the adults have hijacked our world.

"Get ready quickly," Auntie says. "The taxi will be coming at nine o'clock. We'll eat an early breakfast and leave."

"Where are we going?" I say.

"We are returning to Hyderabad. I spoke to your father. He wanted us to come back immediately."

We have a hastily cooked breakfast made with semolina. When I hear the peremptory *pom!pom!,* I take the suitcases down to the taxi and load them into the shabby trunk smelling of petrol and god knows what. Grandma comes up to the car. She looks haggard as if she has aged a good many years since last night.

"Do well at school," Grandma says to us. "Forget about what happened yesterday. You've your entire lives ahead of you."

The taxi makes a three-point turn and rumbles down the road, bouncing over the ruts. Waving for the last time, I look back at Grandma. And in our neighbour's garden, there's a barren spot where the lime tree had once so proudly stood, a glowing totem for its mistress.

That happened a few years ago. People say that going back home is the best part of a journey, but it's not always so, believe me. We were nervous not knowing what our parents' reaction would be. When we got home, Daddy, assuming a stern voice, told us never to take law into our own hands. Mummy interjected with the comment that an eye for an eye was not a solution to the world's problems. In the end, for all the stress Mithuna went through, Daddy bought her another pup—a golden retriever. Mithuna named him 'Whisky'.

30

K
L
A
R
A

D
U

P
L
E
S
S
I
S

Klara du Plessis

Klara du Plessis is a poet residing in Montreal. Her debut collection, *Ekke*, was released from Palimpsest Press, Spring 2018; and her chapbook, *Wax Lyrical*—shortlisted for the bpNichol Chapbook Award—was published by Anstruther Press, 2015. Klara is the editor for *carte blanche*, and currently pursuing a PhD in English Literature.

Essay dwellers

i.

They arrested the windows,
so transparency became a big, gaping hole.

The verbose darkness of metropolitan
public gardens, punished by tiny welts

leaves leave on wet sidewalks.
Vowels age into words.

ii.

Light conditions glorify my life.
I walk into my living room

and it's the Renaissance
halos traipsing around in exercise routines

women with strange round breasts are they tied
with string to bulge forward like mushrooms?

I sit up and listen and wrap the stillness
around my waist. Vanity is healthy.

Women, remember, when
you think you're selfish you're still generous.

I dwell in different kinds of reading:
functional, pleasant, genital.

It's dangerous to be
dependent on walking away from your meaning.

Quidditief

Die gedig wat die dag is.
Die gedig dog aan werklikheid,
maar sienings dink aan gedigte—

(Sommer net)

Quiddity

The daybreak poem.
The poem pondered reality,
but perspectives ponder poems—

(Shooting from the hip)

Immaculate conception

Two egg yolks
quivering in the icebox.
Kinesthetic swag
gold coins
kept together by the thinnest
of film.
Fertile artifacts
two little dots slightly gelatinous
at this point, prick to see
thick yellow nutrition
bulge a drop from the wound.

This way they keep
for a day or two, freshness is key
to art, panting, lapping up
paint with full nouns
like an adult.

Can albumin bleach
the translucent leak
from shaking separation
back and forth plopping
into halved shells, porous white
in a bowl and then the yellows
kept intact for now.
If quick-tempered

the shells are a light way of cracking.
Method acting
your way through life.

Tempera is a technique to paint
with pigments
powders, powder the cheeks
to fill in the blanks of dermis,
powders mixed with yolks
to form a consistency
that endures.
Application has a drier
sheen than oils
a hard shellac
but a fecund being.
Imagine painting in
reproductive cell tissue
ovum mother.
The embryo hidden in a yellow halo
is just another product
of modification, mindless protein
leveled across the canvas
like an insult
to all the babies relaxed
into existence.

A milk

Strange specificity of grammar
hurtling nourishment without prefix, utilitarian

innuendo slipping between action, hand on teat,
and noun, a receptacle watered down

these days to I percent or 2 percent,
normal milk, odour delirious, delicate fluid.

Abnormal milk is the bud of white juice pulsing
from the wound of a flower, clean cut

or the poisonous shrub in a family garden
panicked adults raging against the danger of picking

the white and pink petals kindly.
My editor, who is now my friend, suggests

that the instant of thinking of a poem insinuates
the beginning of writing it and I tend to agree

the sticky note stuck to my wall for half a year
now prompting a milk as a reasonable

topic to write about yellowing not from age
but by the soft chicken colour of the paper

this poem is not what I expected it to be.
Mostly I think of a- as an article, a still life

lent to the table of sentences, but it's
also an appendage, orchestrating grander meanings.

That little surrogate limb meandering
into negation (atheist), approximation (aside, ashore)

novelty (anew), motion (ascend, aspiration)
hopes and dreams passing into the soft outward

collapse of warm air from the lungs
into cold surroundings, lactic breath opacity

Death will desperate

This thing I have for second movements
of classical sonatas, even when
they're not second movements,
but rather the third or the final or the first
in the form of a fantasia.
Strange how movement
here signals containment, a unit of measurement
and not a forward thrust of progression
or it does, but only partly.

I excerpt my listening
bracketing that set of sounds in fixity
while simultaneously letting it exist
in a new form dissociated from closure.
When the composer passes, both releasing
the hold and finalizing the placement of notes,
poor music stuck in the composed
synecdoche of a name while flourishing
in the task of eternity.

Sometimes when words seem
as if they could perform
different functions than they're allotted
I want to grieve the loss
in language invented for the occasion.
I guess that's where voices come in,
tongues, those mythical mechanisms of women

roaring into the future, forging new
ways of continuing.

Continuance which is really a postponement
and not an advance in the sense
of mobility.

To the woodcut above my writing desk

Cecil Skotnes, 1976

Swimmers exercise their way along the bay
low tide excuse to brave the quiet waves
that mark the end of the country. Water soaks up
the beach, bloated, before receding.

The bay twins itself in the mountain, in turn
holding the city, inlay curve, ornamental vessel
of the most basic variety, tectonic chafing, everything
it holds and everything on the reverse side it doesn't hold.

Its taken me twenty years to consider the geographic
specificity of this mountain. Its obvious proximity
to the artist's studio feeds my theory, nestled around
the reservoir where I walk with my friend at the ends of days,

walking with a thrust forward into the distance covered,
our insistence on kilometers rubbing shoulders with aesthetics,
speed, and physical exertion, but the beauty of this body of water
freshwater dactylic surface letting the mountain in sometimes.

Vertical incisions mark the territory of the artwork, shedding
colour, bristling with glee at the periphery of representation.
I look up to this woodcut in the way a wave pretends to be
a mountain for that instant it reaches its cusp, then pretends to be air.

I look up to this woodcut every day, it's a ritual of being
a writer when an artwork hangs above the desk and the desk
is a division which keeps words from falling to the floor.
The artwork betrays my vision into everything.

There's one sharp yellow shard and two thin red cuts
kept apart by a sliver of paper peeking through. These lean
upward into the sky, do not reinstate themselves as sentinels
or sunrays, shimmering in precision. The little white nose

which is also the triangular sail of a boat which is also
a glint of light or a rock bubbling up from the residual depths
of everything only glimpsed in the premise of cutting open
or bulldozing the world into a quiet landscape of exposure.

I ransack my vacancy. Set myself apart from all the holy
mountains I've consumed. The mouth of the river
roils perpendicular to my opinion. Joanne Kyger's mountain ,

its tight poetic gestures dipping into mundane detail.

Etel Adnan's mountain much smaller than expected
on canvas, coloured facets of landscape, pastel nuance.
Ramana Maharshi's mountain , a ventricular coursing,
a cavity landslide dipping through eyes that are

currency for an intermediary in the colour wheel.
Paul Cézanne's mountain fading slowly away, this repetition
called obsession, called passion, called devotion.
Cecil's mountain which is my mountain , it's the one I look

out on even when it's not there or I'm not there because
it is always there. It is my ability to be there that fluctuates.
Sometimes I flare up and realize that the outline we so associate
with my mountain is totally different from other angles.

The relapse is tight, the soft fading into greens and blues
those cold colours chiselling away at the accordance,
the early evening glower into darkness, polite fingers of light
stroking the buttress which is also under renovation.

One wonders at the continued urge to renew, to reach
into the small hearts of the settlements and insinuate dust
as change. Of course there's the potential of rental
if these little outhouses are immaculate, spotless, and unstained

by a capital weakness. A fault line surfaces and plunges
into the crisp details of its own potential for plunder.
Reside here. Grow. Be a protrusion. Shoot from the hip.
Project a collective haemorrhage into the soft expanse

of the present. Plush lapdog mountaineer, sidling
through the underbrush boots first to soften the blow
between earth and heel, ankle elegantly poised to pick
an elegy of flowers

acknowledgements

I would like to acknowledge the hard work from the team that put this anthology together with me. Anna van Valkenburg, this is the second time working with you on a project for Guernica Editions and both times have been a pleasure. Alvin Wong, your enthusiasm and talent motivated me to get my work done so that you could do yours. Khashayar Mohammadi, I am humbled by the amount of work you put in as a volunteer for this project. I would also like to recognize the hard work of Alex Dunn who briefly assisted us at the beginning.

After the ink had dried on the contract, Steven "Takatsu" Lee and I sat down at Knife Fork Book and created a list of 50 authors and spoken word performers we wanted to invite for this anthology. Many said yes, and most submitted work that was accepted. I would like to thank Steven for helping me shape this anthology, the mysterious young lady who joined our conversation without sharing her name and Kirby for creating such a wonderful space.

Michael Mirolla thank you for your bravery. Most publishers would not allow an editor to bring in their own team and have full creative control of such an important project. Also, thank you for being an ear I can bounce my ideas off of, and for your sage advice.

To the people who contributed their writing to this anthology, whether your writing was accepted or not, your hard work is deeply appreciated.

Finally, to the readers of this anthology, I hope that it inspires you to read, write, and be creative in your own way.

acknowledgements

Anthologies ft.diverse/disenfranchised
Canadian voices

#NotYourPrincess, Voices of Native American Women. Lisa Charleyboy, Mary Beth Leatherdale eds. Toronto: Annick Press 2017

A Shapley Fire: Changing the Literary Landscape. Cyril Dabydeen, ed. Oakville: Mosaic Press, 1987

AlliterAsian: anthology of Asian Canadian literature to celebrate 20 years of Ricepaper. Allan Cho ed. Vancouver: Arsenal Pulp Press, 2015

Black Girl Talk. the black girls ed., Toronto: Sister Vision, 1995

Black Notes. Althea Prince ed. Insomniac Press 2017

Black Writing Matters. Whitney French ed. Regina: University of Regina Press 2019

Breathing Fire I. Lorna Crozier, Patrick Lane eds. Pender Harbour: Harbour Publishing, 1995

Breathing Fire 2. Lorna Crozier, Patrick Lane eds. Gibsons: Nightwood Editions, 2004

Calling Cards, New Poetry from Caribbean / Canadian Women. Pamela Mordecai ed. Toronto: Sandberry Press 2005

Dreaming in Indian, Contemporary Native American Voices. Lisa Charleyboy, Mary Beth Leatherdale eds. Toronto: Annick Press 2014

Dykewords, An Anthology of Lesbian writing. The Lesbian Writing and Publishing Collective. Toronto: Women's Press 1999

Fiery Spirits, Canadian Writers Of African Descent. Ayanna Black, ed. Toronto: Harper Collins 1994

Fire On The Water, Volumes One and Two. George Elliott Clarke, ed. Lawrence town Beach: Pottersfield Press 1991

Grammar of Dissent: Poetry and Prose. Carol Morrell, ed. Fredricton NB: Goose Lane Editions, 1994

Impact: Colonialism in Canada. Warren Cariou, Katherena Vermette, Niigaanwewidam James Sinclair eds. Winnipeg: MFNERC 2017

In The Black, New African Canadian Literature. Dr. Althea Prince ed. Insomniac Press, 2012

Indigenous Poetics in Canada, Neal McLeod ed., Wilfred Laurier Press 2012

Making a Difference: Canadian Multicultural Literature. Smaro Kamboureli ed. Toronto: Oxford University Press, 1996.

Manitowapow: Aboriginal Stories from the Land of Water. Warren Cairou ed. Highwater Press 2011

Marvellous Grounds: Queer of Colour Formations in Toronto. Jin Haritaworn, Ghaida Moussa, Syrus Marcus Ware eds. Toronto: Between The Lines 2018

Miscegenation blues : voices of mixed race women. Carol Camper ed. Toronto : Sister Vision 1994.

Native Poetry in Canada - A Contemporary Anthology. Jeannette C. Armstrong, Lally Grauer eds. Peterborough: Broadview Press, 2001

Anthologies ft.diverse/disenfranchised
Canadian voices

Other Tongues: Mixed-Race Women Speak Out. Andrea Thompson, Adebe D.A. eds, Inanna Publications 2011

Over the Rainbow: Folk and Fairy Tales from the Margins. Derek Newman-Stille ed. Exile Editions 2018

Paper Doors: An Anthology of Japanese-Canadian Poetry. Gerry Shikatani, David Aylward eds. David Aylward translator. Toronto: Coach House Press 1981

Plural Desires, Writing Bisexual Women's Realities. The Bisexual Anthology Collective eds. Toronto: Sister Vision 1995

Prison Voices. Lee Weinstein, Richard Jaccoma eds. Kingston: John Howard Society of Canada 2005

Queer View Mirror, Lesbian and Gay Short Short Fiction Vols 1 & 2. James C Johnstone, Karen Tulchinsky eds. Vancouver: Arsenal Pulp Press 1997

Red Silk: An Anthology of South Asian Canadian Women Poets. Rishma Dunlop, Priscilla Uppal eds. Toronto: Mansfield Press 2004.

Returning the gaze : essays on racism, feminism and politics. Himani Bannerji ed. Toronto: Sister Vision 1993.

Siolence, Poets on Women, Violence & Silence. Susan McMaster ed. Quarry Women's Books, 1998

Strike the Wok: An Anthology of Contemporary Chinese Canadian Fiction. Lien Chao, Jim Wong eds. Toronto TSAR Publications 2003

Surviving Canada: Indigenous Peoples Celebrate 150 Years of Betrayal. Kiera L. Ladner & Myra J. Tait eds. Winnipeg: ARP Books 2017

Swallowing Clouds: An Anthology of Chinese Canadian Poetry. Andy Quan, Jim Wong-Chu eds. Vancouver: Arsenal Pulp Press 1999

T Dot Griots: An Anthology of Toronto's Black Storytellers. Steven Green, Karen Richardson eds. Victoria: Trafford Publishing 2004

The Double World, unlisted ed., Toronto: InkWell Workshops (year unavailable)

The Great Black North, Contemporary African Canadian Poetry. Valerie Mason-John, Kevan Anthony Cameron. Calgary: Frontenac House 2013

The Mi'kmaq Anthology Vol 1. Rita Joe, Leslie Choyce eds. Lawrencetown Beach: Pottersfield Press 1997

The Mi'kmaq Anthology Vol 2. Theresa Meuse, Julia Swan, Leslie Choyce eds. Lawrencetown Beach: Pottersfield Press 2011

The New Spice Box, Canadian Jewish Writing Vol 1. Ruth Panofsky ed. Toronto: New Jewish Press 2017

The Next Wave, An Anthology of 21st Century Canadian Poetry. Jim Johnstone ed. Toronto: Anstruther Books 2018

The Unexpected Sky, unlisted ed. Toronto: InkWell Workshops (year unavailable)

The Unpublished City. Dionne Brand ed. Toronto: Book *hug 2017

Anthologies ft.diverse/disenfranchised
Canadian voices

The Unpublished City Vol 2. Dionne Brand, Phoebe Wang, Canisia Lubrin eds.
Toronto: Book *hug 2018

These Pills Don't Come in my Skin Tone. Bassam, Odessia Howlett eds.
Feather and Anchor 2017

Urban Tribes, Native Americans in the City. Lisa Charleyboy,
Mary Beth Leatherdale eds. Toronto: Annick Press

V6A, Writing from Vancouver's Downtown East Side. John Mikhail Asfour,
Elee Kraljii Gardiner eds. Vancouver: Arsenal Pulp Press, 2012

Voices In The Desert: An Anthology of Arabic-Canadian Women Writers.
Elizabeth Dahab ed. Toronto: Guernica Editions, 2002

Voices, Canadian Writers Of African Descent. Ayanna Black, ed. Toronto:
Harper Collins, 1992

W'daub Awae: Speaking True. Warren Cairou ed. Neyaashiinigmiing:
Kegodance Press 2009

We Shall Be Monsters. Derek Newman-Stille ed. Gatineau: Renaissance Book
Press 2018

When Your voice Tastes Like Like Home, Immigrant women Write.Prabhjot
Parmar, Nila Somaia-Carten eds. Second Story Press, 2003

MIX
Paper from
responsible sources
FSC® C100212

Printed in May 2020
by Gauvin Press,
Gatineau, Québec